Summer Beach Bride

SEASIDE DUET

H.Y. HANNA

Books in this Series
Summer Beach Vets: Playing for Love (Book 1)
Summer Beach Vets: Playing to Win (Book 2)
Summer Beach Vets: Playing by Heart (Book 3)
Summer Beach Vets: Playing the Fool (Book 4)
Summer Beach Bride: Seaside Duet (Book 5)

YOU ARE CORDIALLY INVITED
TO CELEBRATE THE WEDDING OF:

Sara Monroe
&
Craig Murray

SEASIDE DUET

SUMMER BEACH BRIDE

DANCING & RECEPTION
(AND DRAMA & ROMANCE!) TO FOLLOW

RSVP: hyhanna.com/newsletter   DRESS CODE: BEACH WEAR

CONTENTS

CHAPTER ONE

Natalie looked up from the glossy brochures. *What was that burning smell?* Her eyes widened as she saw the smoke wafting from the kitchen doorway

"Argh!"

She dropped the brochures and ran into the kitchen. The toaster was smouldering, a thick plume of black smoke rising from its vents. She jumped forwards and yanked the plug from the wall, then eyed the toaster again warily. No flames. Whew. She'd got here just in time.

Oh no, the smoke alarm... Natalie glanced up at the ceiling anxiously. If it went off, it would definitely wake up Gran.

She threw open the kitchen windows, then grabbed a tea towel and began waving it frantically in all directions, trying to disperse the smoke. She waited tensely, but no piercing wail filled the air and, after a moment, Natalie began to relax. Still, just to be safe, she went through to the living room and opened all the windows there as well.

The creak of a bicycle brake made her glance out of the windows. It was Graham the postie stopping by their mailbox. He rearranged his post bag, then looked up and saw her.

He sniffed the air. "Burnt the brekkie again, eh, Natalie?" he called out, grinning.

She grinned back at him. "Can you smell it from there?"

"What are you doing up so early anyhow?"

"Going for a run on the beach before I start work."

"Your Gran told me you got that new job at the resort—congratulations."

Natalie nodded. "Thanks. It's not totally in the bag, though. I've got to get through the trial period first, you know. But if I can pull off this wedding..."

Graham smiled reassuringly. "No worries, you'll do it. Reckon if anybody can pull off our first celebrity wedding in Summer Beach, it's you."

Natalie smiled and looked at the older man fondly. It was lovely to have someone show such fatherly pride in her. She couldn't remember a time when Graham hadn't been there to start her day, as much a part of the morning routine as breakfast and brushing your teeth.

"There's a card here for you," said Graham, nodding at the mailbox. "Come all the way from the U.S."

Natalie stiffened, but she kept her smile in place. "Thanks, Graham. I'll be out in a minute to get it."

She waved him off and stood at the windows for a long time after he had gone, staring into space. Finally, she remembered the time and forced herself to go outside to the mailbox. Back in the kitchen, she sorted quickly through the pile of letters, bills, and leaflets, pausing only when she came to the thick cream envelope. Her name and address were written across the front in a familiar bold, dark handwriting. She didn't even glance at the U.S. address in the top left-hand corner. Instead, she turned and threw the card straight into the bin. Then she pushed the rest of the mail to the other side of the counter and turned back to deal with the charred mess inside the toaster.

Twenty minutes later, Natalie was on the road in her old Holden Barina, cruising down the coastal drive towards Summer Beach Resort. It had been a pretty mild winter so far and she hoped fervently that the good weather would continue. *At least until next week and the wedding*, she thought, mentally crossing her fingers. Australia was famous for its sunshine—even in the middle of winter—and this was the one time she needed it to live up to its reputation.

She glanced out the windows as the road curved.

3

The bush thinned out by the verge to show the spectacular coastline on her right: golden sand stretching for miles in either direction, edged with turquoise blue waters and foaming white waves. Natalie felt her heart give that familiar tug every time she saw the ocean. She had grown up here and yet still she never quite got used to the beauty of this unspoilt corner of the New South Wales coast.

Suddenly she couldn't wait to get down there—feel the sand between her toes, the sea breeze on her face. Her thoughts returned briefly to the morning post and her face clouded over, then she pushed the card from her mind and focused on her run instead. Yes, some time on the beach was exactly what she needed to clear her mind and set her up for the day.

When Natalie arrived, the resort still had that hushed, early morning feel, although she was surprised to see a fair number of guests milling about the lobby already. It looked like business was booming. *Ellie will be pleased*, she thought with a smile, knowing how hard the resort's PR Manager had worked in the last month to generate buzz and gain media exposure for the grand opening. As the first luxury resort on this part of the coast, the success of this place meant a lot to Summer Beach—bringing in tourists, providing jobs, and helping to put this idyllic little seaside town on the map.

And building my future too, thought Natalie as she turned down the private hallway which led to the wing that housed the resort administration offices. Getting the title of Event Coordinator for such a prestigious luxury resort would be a huge boost to her C.V. and would really help launch her career.

She dropped off her handbag and a change of clothes in her office, then hurried out towards the back of the forty-acre property. A sprawling landscaped bush garden rolled out towards the water's edge. Private luxury villas and other resort amenities like tennis courts, a health spa, gourmet restaurants, and shopping boutiques were cleverly hidden amongst the foliage, whilst a giant lagoon pool took pride of place in the middle of the rear gardens. Beyond it, the carefully cultivated wilderness merged into soft white sand as the land sloped down towards the sea. It was the perfect combination of conscious design and natural disarray.

A few guests were already out claiming deckchairs around the pool and farther out towards the sea, laying towels down on the sand. Natalie walked down to the beach and along it until she reached the edge of the main resort area. The private beach stretched beyond here for another two kilometres and she smiled as she took in the view in front of her: a long strip of white sand narrowing to the horizon—hemmed on the right by the blue waters of the Pacific Ocean and on the left by a rise of undulating sand dunes.

Natalie breathed deeply, savouring the salty sea air. There were many perks that came with her new job and one of the best was access to this private section of shoreline. Not that any of the public beaches around Summer Beach were that busy, but it was hard to beat a strip of paradise right on her office door step!

It's not my office yet, Natalie reminded herself. She still had to prove herself; she had been lucky even to be considered for the role. She had sent in her application, not really expecting to get any response, and had been pleasantly surprised when they called her in for an interview. After all, a luxury five-star resort like this could hire any number of experienced event coordinators—why would they pick a beginner like her?

But it seemed that the board of Summer Beach Resort was sticking to its promise of giving back to the local community. They were keen to hire as many of their staff from the local towns as they could and Natalie had jumped at the opportunity, doing everything she could to impress at the interview. She may not have had much experience, but she more than made up for it with determination and enthusiasm.

Well, it must have worked. They'd agreed to a trial period to see her in action. Now, if she could just impress them with results, she knew she stood a good chance of getting the position. And everything hinged on this wedding...

Natalie felt a flutter of anxiety. It was an important job—not only a celebrity wedding, but one which would help to enhance the resort's image—and hardly the kind of thing for a novice like her to tackle. Was she taking on more than she could handle? But she liked a challenge—and so far, the preparations were under control. Besides, Craig and Sara were such a lovely couple—even if her job hadn't depended on it, she would have wanted to do everything to enhance their special day.

And if I stand here daydreaming much longer, I won't get anything done! Natalie chided herself. She kicked off her sandals and tucked them beside a small rock, then broke into a slow run. *There's nothing like running barefoot on the beach*, Natalie thought, savouring the feel of the sand between her toes. She veered slightly, running along the water's edge, but keeping just out of reach of the waves. Her legs pounded faster, leaving a trail of footprints on the wet sand behind her. A spray of seawater caught her in the face and she tasted salt on her lips. The sun sparkled on the water and, at the horizon, the blue green of the sea merged into a cloudless sky. It was the perfect morning.

Her calves were beginning to ache now and Natalie slowed, her breathing heavy. She had come much farther than she had anticipated—she was almost at the end of the private section of the beach. Up ahead, she could see the line of rocks that stretched out into the sea, in a sort of natural pier, with the waves crashing and breaking against the tip.

Wait...

Natalie realised that the water splashing in the distance was not waves breaking on the rocks. Somebody was out there, thrashing around in the water near the rocks. A man.

She heard a cry of pain, abruptly cut off as his head submerged. For a heart-stopping second, he didn't come back up, then his head broke the surface again, and he coughed and choked as he struggled in the water.

Natalie didn't hesitate. She plunged into the surf, wading out as far she could until the sand fell away from beneath her feet, then kicking strongly as she swam out towards the man. She grabbed his arm and began hauling him back towards the shore. They staggered together out of the water and he dropped to his knees on the sand, then rolled over onto his back, gasping and panting.

Natalie dropped to her knees next to him and her eyes went immediately to the angry red welts on his left leg. Her heart sank as she recognised the marks.

Jellyfish stings.

CHAPTER TWO

"Aaaah!" The man reached forwards, his face grimacing in pain.

"No, don't touch it!" Natalie grabbed his hand. "The tentacles are still embedded in your skin. If you touch them, you'll just get stung more." She pushed him gently back onto the sand. "You need to keep still, otherwise the capsules will release more toxin... Don't move! Just stay there!"

She ran back to the water's edge and scooped up some seawater in her hands, then went back to the man and doused his leg with the salty solution. He flinched and gritted his teeth. She repeated this a few times more, then paused to examine his leg again.

"Did you see what kind of jellyfish it was?" Natalie asked, not looking up.

"No…" he gasped. "Didn't even know there were jellyfish in the water. Why? Does it matter?"

"It does if it's a box jellyfish. You need to get to hospital immediately for some anti-venom. But if it's a bluebottle or a Jimble, you should be okay—"

"*Okay?* I feel like my leg's been permanently Tasered! And what are you doing with the seawater? I thought you're supposed to put vinegar on a jellyfish sting."

Natalie shook her head impatiently. "Only if it's a box jellyfish. Otherwise the vinegar can actually make things worse. That's why I asked. Salt water is the safest—it'll still neutralise the stingers." She looked urgently around. "What we really need is something to scrape off the tentacles. They'll keep firing unless we can get them off."

She spied a large limpet shell a few feet away and hurried to pick it up, then returned to the man's side and put a gentle hand on his shoulder.

"I'm sorry—this is going to hurt, but I've got to do this."

He nodded. Natalie bit her lip, leaned over and, using the sharp flattened edge of the shell, carefully scraped the skin over the affected area. He flinched slightly and she saw his hands clench until his knuckles went white, but he didn't cry out. She felt a flicker of admiration for him. She had been stung herself as a child and knew that nothing came close to the white-hot burning pain of a jellyfish sting.

At last, she had scraped off as much of the

tentacles as she could see. She eased back slowly and gave him an encouraging smile.

"I think that's done it. The pain will still be bad for a while, but you're probably not in any danger—if this had been a box jellyfish, you'd be going into heart failure by now."

He breathed out slowly, relaxing slightly. "Thanks. It's easing a bit."

Natalie glanced at him, then rocked back slightly on her heels in surprise. It was the first time she had looked at him—*really* looked at him—and she caught her breath as she took in the dark wavy hair, chiselled cheekbones, and strong jaw covered faintly with designer stubble. He had eyes the colour of heather—a mix of green and grey—fringed by the most amazingly thick lashes and crinkling at the corners, as if he laughed a lot. He was wearing surf shorts which showed his toned, athletic body to perfection, with droplets of seawater clinging to the lean muscles of his arms and the hard planes of his chest and stomach.

Natalie realised that she was staring and hastily looked away. She cleared her throat. "You still need to get some first aid—some painkillers, ice, and bandages."

"Dammit, there should be signs warning swimmers to be careful in the water."

She looked back at him and said dryly, "I sort of guessed from your accent, but... I take it you're not from here? This is Australia. You *always* have to be careful in the water."

"Yeah, I'm learning that lesson the hard way," he said with a rueful grin. "I'm American. I'm staying at the resort." He held his hand out. "My name's Ben."

Natalie hesitated, then put her hand into his. "I'm Natalie." His clasp was strong and warm, and she felt a tingle of awareness between her fingers. She pulled her hand quickly from his.

"We should get you back to the resort and—" She paused as she saw the blood on his ankle. "Oh! You've been cut!"

He followed her gaze and winced. "Must have been when I was thrashing around near those rocks. I probably kicked one that was underwater. Have to say, the pain from the jellyfish stings was so bad, I didn't even notice this until now..."

Natalie leaned over and peered gingerly at the wound. It was a deep gash, with blood oozing freely. "You'll have to get this properly cleaned—you might even need stitches. And a tetanus shot and some antibiotics. You can't be too careful with cuts at the beach, especially with shellfish around."

She stood up and helped him to his feet. He was easily six feet and towered over her. Natalie felt his arm go around her shoulders and let him lean into her as she put her own arm around him. At any other time, she might have felt self-conscious, but somehow it felt perfectly natural to support him as he began hobbling back up the beach. He smelled of salt and sea and some undefinable clean, male scent. She had never been so aware of someone as she was of this handsome stranger.

By the time they reached the resort, she could see what the effort had cost him—his jaw was clenched and there were beads of sweat on his forehead—but he said nothing, just giving her a strained smile. Again, she felt that flicker of admiration for him.

Within minutes of arriving back in the landscaped area by the pool, they were surrounded by staff, including the resort manager who paled when he saw Ben's injuries. While it was hardly the resort's fault, it would not be good publicity for any guest to be badly injured during the opening month. He was relieved to see that it wasn't a box jellyfish attack, but hurriedly agreed that a visit to the local hospital emergency ward was essential.

"Our chauffeur is out picking up a guest at the moment and I don't have my car with me today," he said apologetically. "A taxi might take too long. But don't worry, I'll get one of the staff to take you—"

"I'll do it," Natalie volunteered.

The manager turned eagerly to her. "Would you, Natalie? That would be great. I wouldn't need to get someone to cover for you."

They waited until an ice pack had been applied to the stings and a makeshift bandage wrapped around the cut foot, then Ben hobbled after her to her car. Natalie drove as fast as she dared. She was relieved to find the Emergency Department relatively empty when they arrived. They whisked Ben away and she didn't see him again until nearly an hour later—when he limped back into the waiting area with his foot securely wrapped in a fresh bandage.

"Almost as good as new," he said with a smile. "No stitches, but I've got to keep it clean and covered. Should be fine in a couple of days. And the stings are calming down too."

"That's great news." Natalie returned his smile, then led the way back out to the car park.

"I'm sorry, this has all been a pain for you— hanging around, waiting for me..." he said as they pulled out of the car park and headed back towards the resort.

"No worries, it's fine." Natalie glanced at him. "You're looking a lot better," she added shyly.

"Yeah, they gave me some powerful painkillers. I'm feeling pretty awesome right now, like I could do anything! I'm sure I'll change my mind later when they wear off." He chuckled, then looked at her curiously. "So... you work at the resort? I guessed from what the manager said."

Natalie nodded. "Don't worry. My hours are pretty flexible. I can catch up on work later tonight."

"I was actually hoping you might have dinner with me later tonight—as a sort of thank you— although I have a feeling now that I'm going to be knocked out from all this medication. Maybe tomorrow—"

"It's no biggie," said Natalie quickly. "Don't feel that you need to—"

"I don't." He looked at her, a smile in his eyes. "I'd *like* to have dinner with you. The rescue was just a convenient excuse."

There was an awkward silence in the car and Natalie felt warm colour come to her cheeks. She turned her eyes back on the road and concentrated on her driving, trying to think of how to answer.

Did she *want* to have dinner with him?

Yes, she did. In fact, what frightened her was how *much* she wanted to, how hard her heart had jumped when he had asked, how warm she'd felt when he looked at her with that twinkle in his grey-green eyes...

What was going on? Sure, he was drop-dead gorgeous, but she wasn't the type of girl to drool over hot guys. If anything, she was pretty wary of romantic entanglements. But she had never felt this instant connection with any other man before. So far, they had barely exchanged more than a few words—and mostly about jellyfish, she thought wryly—and yet already she was feeling a strange ease with him.

"Hey, look, it's okay, if you don't really want to—"

"No, it's not that..." She darted a quick glance at him. "I mean..." She took a deep breath. *Oh, why the hell not? What am I afraid of?* She gave him a smile. "Thanks—that would be nice."

"Great. Shall we meet in the lobby tomorrow night—say, seven o'clock?"

"Okay."

Suddenly, Natalie felt inexplicably shy. She turned her eyes on the road again, then—desperate to ease the awkward atmosphere—she reached for the radio and switched it on. The sounds of a familiar guitar riff filled the car. It was the opening chords of "Sweet Home Alabama". Slowly, Natalie began to relax, finding the familiar strains of the melody soothing and distracting. Without realising it, she began to hum along to the music under her breath.

Ben was obviously enjoying it too. He was tapping his toe and nodding his head in time to the music. He reached forwards suddenly for the volume dial.

"Awesome song... mind if I turn it up?"

Natalie shook her head, secretly pleased. It was what she had been wanting to do. He whacked the volume right up. She felt a thrill of exhilaration as the song filled the car. She had never driven like this, with the music at full blast, ringing in her ears and her pulse pounding to the bass rhythm of the melody. She laughed out loud in spite of herself.

"It's great, isn't it?" said Ben, grinning. Then he opened his mouth and began to sing along to the music.

Natalie felt her heart flip over in her chest. He had an amazing voice—a deep, sexy baritone that seemed to touch something in the deepest part of her. She glanced at him, then before she realised what she was doing, she was singing with him— singing at the top of her lungs as they sped down the coastal road. She had never felt like this before—so exhilarated, so alive, so *free*. By the time they turned into the resort entrance and the song was coming to its end, her cheeks were flushed and her eyes were sparkling.

Ben turned towards her. "You have a beautiful voice," he said. "Have you ever considered singing professionally?"

It was as if he had thrown cold water over her. Natalie clamped her mouth shut. Her hands tightened on the steering wheel and she turned her face away from him.

"No."

Suddenly, the car seemed too small, the music too loud, pressing in on her from all sides. She reached out and lowered the volume on the radio, then she wound down the window and took a deep breath of fresh air. From the corner of her eye, she saw Ben look at her quizzically, but he didn't make a comment. The car slid to a stop at last in front of the main resort entrance.

Natalie said, "You can get out first. I have to take the car round to park it on the other side—but this will save you the walk."

Ben looked at her with a puzzled frown, but she kept her face averted and would not meet his eyes.

Finally, he gave a nod and said, "Okay, thanks for the ride... and for everything."

"You're welcome."

He gave her another look, then opened the door and got out. She kept her gaze straight ahead until he had slammed the door, then she allowed herself a quick glance in his direction. He was making his way slowly into the lobby. Even walking with a slight limp, he had more presence than any other man around. She saw several women's eyes lingering on Ben as he passed.

Natalie tore her gaze away from him and swung the steering wheel savagely, turning the car towards the staff car park.

CHAPTER THREE

"Oh God, I look so fat in this." Sara Monroe stared at her reflection in horror.

"You do *not* look fat. You look gorgeously curvy," said Ellie as she watched from the chair beside the mirror.

"This dress was a mistake," said Sara wildly. "I don't know what I was thinking, going for this look with a figure like mine—"

"What are you talking about? You look fantastic! You *need* a figure with curves like yours to do that dress justice."

Sara looked uncertainly at her reflection and wished for the hundredth time that she had her cousin Ellie's confidence. They were both blessed with fuller figures, but whilst Ellie embraced her curves with the fierce pride of an Amazonian warrior princess, Sara felt constantly self-conscious about her fuller hips and thighs. It hadn't helped that, until recently, she had lived in L.A. where body image was the No. 1 obsession, and she had had first-hand experience of how cruelly the media could treat women with less than perfect catwalk-model figures.

Now she looked at the ivory silk sheath gown, with the empire line bodice and flowing train, and all she could see was the bulge of her hips and the way the fabric clung to her thighs. How could she have allowed herself to be talked into this gown for her wedding? *Because Craig loved it*, a little voice reminded her. Her fiancé had broken with tradition and come wedding dress shopping with her—and when he had seen her step out in this dress, the look in his eyes had said everything. She had felt like the most beautiful woman in the world.

As if reading her thoughts, Ellie shook her head impatiently and said, "Craig thinks you look gorgeous and that's all that matters, isn't it?"

"Not that he's unbiased, of course," muttered Sara, smoothing her hands down over her hips.

"No, you're right—he thinks you look gorgeous in everything," said Ellie, grinning. "Even though in reality you're a huge, fat hag. Good thing you found a man with such poor eyesight, huh?"

Sara looked around for something to throw at her cousin, but she couldn't help the corners of her mouth tugging up in a reluctant smile. "Okay, okay, maybe I'm being stupid. I just feel... I don't know... so unsure about the wedding!"

Ellie frowned. "You're not unsure about marrying Craig, are you?"

"No, of course not," said Sara quickly. "It's just... I don't know—I was so excited when Craig proposed and I couldn't wait for us to get married. But now this wedding... I feel so overwhelmed by it all... and starting the new job... and Mom and Dad and the family coming over from the States... and then the media interest here in Australia—"

"Relax! It'll be fine," said Ellie. "Besides, I thought you're getting Natalie on board?"

Sara's face brightened. "Yeah. That's going to be a big help having her take over the preparations. I was nuts to think I could do everything myself."

"I'm sure she's going do a great job," said Ellie with an approving nod. "I was pretty impressed at her interview. They got me to sit in because the event coordinator will be working closely with the PR department for a lot of things... Natalie hasn't got a lot of experience yet, but she's really enthusiastic and keen to try out new stuff."

"That's what I thought when I met her," Sara agreed. "That's why I hired her, even though she's never organised a wedding before." She smiled. "To be honest, I just really liked her."

"Me too."

"We're having our second meeting with her tomorrow morning. Just to go over everything properly so she can check what I've done so far and what she needs to take over."

"Oh, make sure she remembers to prepare for heavy breezes down on the waterfront. I was doing some research on beach weddings and that's a major issue. You know, like weighing down the programmes or maybe even using something else instead of paper. And candles! Are you going to have candles? If you're doing the ceremony just before sunset, they'll look really nice, but you'll have to put them in hurricane lamps otherwise they'll get blown out. And what about..."

Sara glanced at Ellie and hid a smile. Her cousin was taking over in her typical perfectionist, micro-managing fashion. It was ironic that Ellie had told her to relax—if Ellie was this bad now, she shuddered to think what her cousin would be like when it came to planning her own wedding!

"... and have you thought about the cake? I'm worried about cream icing melting down on the beach—although, I suppose since we're in winter now, it won't be too hot." Ellie shook her head and smiled. "You know, I've been living in Australia for nearly a year and I still can't get over it being mid-winter in July. Things really are upside-down here. It's kinda strange to think about everyone back home going to 4th of July celebrations and pool parties and having a barbie—"

Sara laughed. "It sounds to me like you're turning Aussie already. Did you hear yourself just now? 'Having a barbie'... when was the last time you said 'barbecue' properly?"

Ellie gave a sheepish smile. "I even caught myself saying 'arvo' yesterday instead of 'afternoon'."

"Seriously?" Sara laughed again. "Okay, just as long as you don't start calling me 'mate'."

"I love it when I hear my two favourite Americans speak Strine. Nothing as sexy as 'mate' in an American accent," a deep voice said in amusement.

They turned quickly to see a head poking around the edge of the curtains enclosing the changing area.

"Craig!" Sara said, her face breaking into a wide smile as she looked at the handsome veterinarian who had captured her heart. With his deep blue eyes, square-jawed good looks, and tall, muscular figure, it was easy to see why Craig was a national heartthrob. As the star of the hit TV show, *Aussie Beach Vet*, he was a favourite household name and had been voted "Sexiest TV Celebrity" for several years running.

And he chose me. Sara still felt like she had to pinch herself sometimes. She knew that she was the envy of every woman in Australia. It was over six months now, but she still couldn't believe how her whirlwind vacation romance had turned into this fairy-tale ending.

I haven't got to the fairy-tale ending yet though, Sara reminded herself. But seeing Craig made her feel calmer and more confident that everything was going to be okay.

"It's great to see you, but what are you doing here?" she asked.

"I finished work early. The last case was cancelled. Dog with a bowel obstruction—I thought I was going to have to operate, but he passed it at the last moment."

"It's not Milo, is it?" asked Ellie, standing up with a worried look on her face.

Craig gave a wry smile. "No, that cheeky Lab hasn't eaten anything he shouldn't this week... yet." He stepped through the curtains. "But speaking of Milo: I saw him and Will in town on my way here. Will was looking for you. He wanted to know if you were still coming to his after-school 'Munch and Move' contest."

"Oh, my God, yes—I almost forgot!" said Ellie, scrambling to grab her handbag from the chair. "I'm really sorry, Sara, but you don't mind me leaving you, do you? I promised Will I'd be there."

Sara gave her an incredulous look. "You're going to something called 'Munch and Move' with a bunch of primary kids?"

Ellie gave a sheepish grin. "Yeah, I thought it might be fun. Anyway, see you guys later!"

Craig watched Ellie leave, then turned and said, "You know, when I first met Ellie, I used to wonder if all Americans were so uptight! She's changed a lot. It's really nice to see her chill out more. Not that she wasn't nice before," he added hastily. "But it's good to see her let her hair down and have a bit of fun."

Sara giggled. "Yeah, if you'd told me a year ago that Ellie would be spending most of her free time running around with a nine-year-old boy and his drooling Labrador, I'd have said you were out of your mind. But it's been so good for her. It's like—it brings out a different side to her I've never seen. And when you watch her with Milo, you'd never believe that she hated dogs before."

"Gotta give Dan some credit too, eh?" said Craig teasingly, referring to his partner at the animal hospital.

Sara smiled. Dr Dan O'Brien was the first man to get under her workaholic cousin's defences. They were such opposites you'd never have thought that they could even *like* each other, much less fall in love. But it had been wonderful seeing Ellie with Dan and how he'd shown her that life didn't have to be perfectly under control for you to be happy.

"Yes, it's amazing what love can do."

"Would you like to remind me?" Craig gave her a wicked grin, coming closer to draw her into his arms.

"Craig! The dress!" Sara protested, trying to hold him at arm's length.

"Hey, this is for a beach wedding, right? We've got to make sure it can withstand a bit of rough handling..." he said with a twinkle in his eye.

Then he lowered his head and captured her

lips—and Sara forgot about the dress, the wedding, everything. Craig kissed her with a passionate intensity that made every nerve ending in her body tingle and Sara sighed dreamily when he finally released her. The sound of someone clearing their throat made them both jump.

"Everything all right?" asked the manager of the bridal boutique with a knowing smile.

"Er... yes," said Sara, blushing as she stepped away from Craig. "The alterations look good. The train is a much better length now."

The manager smiled. "Fantastic. I'll have the final touches added to the beadwork and embroidery on the bodice and it'll be ready early next week. Have you decided on the head piece or veil that you will be wearing with it?"

Sara bit her lip. "I'm not sure yet. It depends on how I'm going to do my hair. I've got an appointment with the hairstylist tomorrow afternoon."

"No worries. You can always pop back in and select something later in the week. Well, I'll leave you to get changed."

She left and the curtains fluttered after her. Sara turned away and began unzipping her dress, but paused as Craig put a hand on her arm.

"Actually, Sara, I wanted to speak to you about something."

She looked at him, slightly worried by his serious tone.

"I've been approached by the production company who run my *Aussie Beach Vet* show. They want to do a special feature on our wedding."

"*Our wedding?*"

"Yes, you know—a sort of reality TV type documentary. Nothing too slick, maybe just a cameraman following you around in the last week during the preparations and then coverage on the day itself. They want it to be sort of intimate and casual—almost like home video—so that the viewers can feel like they're experiencing the wedding with us."

Sara felt a flash of annoyance. "It's *our* wedding. It's a private thing. I don't want half of Australia looking over my shoulder, 'experiencing it with me'!" She gave him a frustrated look. "Craig, you know how I feel about media attention. I can't believe you're even asking this—"

"I know, I know..." He held his hands up in a gesture of surrender. "But you see, the thing is, people love celebrity weddings and the media are willing to pay big money for exclusive coverage of the event."

He named a figure which made Sara gasp.

Craig nodded. "Yeah, they're willing to pay that and a bonus once the show is aired—and I could donate it all to charity." He took a step closer to her and said earnestly, "Look, Sara, I know how you feel about publicity and media attention; I know you don't like the celebrity aspect of life with me... and I totally understand it, given what you went through back in the States. But I feel like this is one area where celebrities can use their power to do some real good. It's a way to give back. We could raise a lot of money for a really good cause."

"I—" Sara hesitated.

She felt torn. She already found it a huge challenge dealing with paparazzi following her and Craig whenever they were out in public places. She hated seeing herself in various celebrity magazines. It brought back the whole nightmare of what had happened back in L.A. when she had been made a laughing stock of the whole country by her ex-boyfriend, actor Jeff Kingston. The last thing she wanted was more cameras covering her every move on the biggest day of her life.

She looked pleadingly at Craig. "I'd imagined a small, intimate beach wedding, with close friends and family... Not some crazy celebrity event with cameras everywhere and—"

"But it won't be that!" said Craig. "I've told them that we're not having a big society wedding. It is just going to be a small affair—"

"A small affair that'll be broadcast across national TV," said Sara sarcastically.

Craig sighed. "If you really feel that you can't do it, I'll tell them no. I just thought... Bloody hell, there's going to be intense media interest in our wedding anyway—I'll bet the paps will find a way to crash the wedding and get shots of us whether you like it or not. Why don't we take that power back into our hands? Get them on our side and direct them to the shots we want—*and* get them to donate to a good cause while we're at it."

Sara swallowed. Craig was right—it wasn't as if they could hide away from the media. This morning already she had seen a photographer taking her picture as she arrived outside the bridal boutique. She had no doubt the photo would be appearing in this weekend's celebrity magazine. Doing a deal for official media coverage would be a good way to take control *and* raise money for a good cause.

Besides... She glanced at Craig from beneath her lashes. She could see that this was important to him. Was she being selfish? She felt a stab of guilt. This amazing man asked so little of her—and the one time he asked for something important to him, she was kicking up a fuss.

She took a deep breath. "All right. I... I'll do it."

"You mean it?" Craig's face broke into a broad smile.

Sara nodded, hoping that she wouldn't regret her decision.

"Great. I'll go ring my agent now." He leaned over and dropped a kiss on her forehead. "I'll see you outside."

As he turned to push his way through the curtains, Sara called out:

"Craig, you haven't forgotten that we're meeting Natalie Walker tomorrow morning, ten o'clock at the resort? She's the new event coordinator and she's taking over the preparations for the wedding."

Craig raised an amused eyebrow. "I'm surprised Ellie is willing to let anyone else in on this. This wedding has always been her baby—I don't think she could have obsessed over the details more if it had been her own wedding."

Sara laughed. "I know. But Ellie really likes Natalie and thinks she'll do an awesome job. And so do I."

"Well, I'm looking forward to meeting her. Should be good to get someone else on board. Don't worry— I've got Dan to cover surgery for me tomorrow morning, so I'll just be catching up on some post-operative admin. I'll be there at ten o'clock."

"Oh, and have you thought any more about the music? Natalie will be wanting to know about that. I suppose we need to go and see some bands or listen to their demos—"

"Don't worry about the music," said Craig "I've got something organised already."

Sara raised her eyebrows. "You never told me. Have you picked a band? Who is it?"

Craig gave a mysterious smile. "It's a surprise. You'll find out more tomorrow."

CHAPTER FOUR

Natalie sighed as she shut the front door and kicked off her shoes. It had been a long day. There had been that big Japanese tourist group excursion, the Royal Society of Pathologists' convention, the young mother's yoga retreat, and the local businessman's awards luncheon to organise, not to mention Craig and Sara's wedding preparations. She had stayed late to check the resort's banquet menus and research the local florists she could use. She wanted to be fully prepared for their meeting tomorrow morning.

"Gran, I'm home!" she called, dropping her handbag on the sofa and making her way into the kitchen.

It was empty. She frowned. It was almost a shock not seeing her grandmother standing at the kitchen sink or busily stirring something at the stove. For as long as she could remember, coming home from school or work had always meant stepping into a house filled with the homely smells of cooking and baking, the sound of *Neighbours* on the TV in the background, and the comforting bustle of her grandmother's presence.

Now the kitchen felt so cold and empty, the house eerily silent.

"Gran?"

Natalie wandered down the hallway and out onto the rear deck. She saw her grandmother immediately. Rita Walker was lying on a deckchair underneath the old gum tree. She must have fallen asleep while reading a book: she was slumped over to one side, with her head on a shoulder and an open paperback on her lap.

Natalie was struck by how small her grandmother looked. She always thought of her as a busy, capable woman, there to offer wise words and warm hugs, cooking, cleaning, giving Natalie equal measures of tough love and doting patience. But now she saw, for the first time, that her grandmother was getting old. There were deep lines on her face… and when had her hair become so grey? Her body looked frail and shrunken, lying there slack against the deckchair.

Natalie felt a sudden wave of fear grip her. For the first time, she thought about what it would be like if her grandmother was gone and she would be left alone in the world. She had no other family. It had always been just her and Gran. The thought of being on her own was suddenly terrifying.

Rita stirred and opened her eyes. She blinked and squinted across the yard. "Natalie?"

"Yes, Gran." Natalie felt a sense of relief on hearing the familiar voice. She hurried down the steps leading down from the deck and crossed over to her grandmother's side.

"I must have fallen asleep…" Rita yawned. "Have you just got back?"

Natalie nodded.

"You left so early this morning, I didn't even get a chance to see you."

"I wanted to hit the beach before the day started."

"Good run?" Her grandmother smiled at her.

Natalie hesitated. Summer Beach was a small place. Someone was bound to have seen her and Ben at the hospital. Word would get back to Gran and she'd would wonder why Natalie hadn't mentioned it. *Anyway, why* shouldn't *I mention it? It's not like anything happened. Not that I was* expecting *anything, of course—or even thought about it—or—*

"Natalie?"

Natalie gave a start and realised that her grandmother was looking at her curiously. She pulled her thoughts together.

"Actually, this funny thing happened. There was a guy—a guest at the resort—who was having trouble in the water. He had a run-in with a stinger. I helped him out and took him to the hospital."

"Bloody Nora, you serious?" Rita sat up in the deck chair. "Was he all right? What did the medicos say? It wasn't a box, was it?"

"He's fine," Natalie reassured her. "No, it was a bluey, I think. The tentacles hurt like heck, but I managed to get most of them off at the beach. He'd cut his foot as well so he got that bandaged at the ED."

"Poor bugger." Rita shook her head. "Was he a tourist? Hope it wasn't his first day in Oz or something…"

"He took it quite well, actually. But yes, he's American."

"Old bloke?"

"No, he was a young guy. Late twenties, maybe? A couple of years older than me, I think. His name was Ben…" For some reason, Natalie felt her cheeks reddening. She hoped fervently that the falling twilight would make it hard to see. Her grandmother had really sharp eyes.

Rita looked at Natalie thoughtfully. But to the latter's relief, she didn't comment. She just yawned again and said, "What time is it?"

"Nearly seven o'clock."

"Oh my goodness, I must be getting on with dinner!" Rita grasped the arms of the deckchair to heave herself up. Then she flinched and sat back down again, grimacing in pain.

"Gran? What's the matter?" asked Natalie in alarm.

"Nothing, nothing…" Rita gave a wan smile. "Just my hip acting up." She patted Natalie's arm. "Don't worry, it'll be fine in a minute."

"It's not fine!" said Natalie in frustration. "You should've had that op months ago! I don't know what the hospital was thinking, putting you on a waiting list—"

"There are lots of other people just like me, also on the waiting list," said Rita gently. "I just have to wait my turn."

"But it's not good enough!" said Natalie, unexpected tears springing to her eyes. "What if you get worse? What if something really bad happens? What if you—" She broke off suddenly, turning her face away.

"Hey, hey…" Rita reached out and caught her hand. "What's going on, possum?"

At the sound of her childhood nickname, Natalie felt the lump in her throat grow even bigger. She blinked rapidly and swallowed.

"Nothing. Sorry, I think I've just had a really long day…" She gave a shaky laugh. "I just hate to see you suffer, Gran."

"Don't worry about me. A couple of painkillers and I'll be fine. Just give me a moment…" Rita grasped the arms of her deckchair again and slowly pushed herself to her feet. She grimaced again, but managed to stand this time. Natalie sprang up to help her, but her grandmother shook her off.

"Don't fuss. I'll be fine." Rita took a couple of experimental steps, then began walking slowly back to the house.

"Forget the cooking tonight, Gran," said Natalie, following her. "I can just order us some Thai takeaway…"

"You eat too much of that foreign stuff," said Rita, making a face. "All those weird dishes with fish sauce and tofu and portaloos and God knows what else…"

"It's *vindaloo*, Gran," said Natalie, giggling.

This was one thing where she and her beloved grandmother didn't see eye to eye. Natalie loved Australia's multicultural character and the chance it gave her to easily sample different exotic dishes, but her grandmother had steadfastly refused to try any foreign cuisine, no matter how hard Natalie tried to cajole her. The most adventurous Rita had ever got was when she agreed to go with Natalie to the Chinese down in Summer Beach village for Natalie's twenty-fourth birthday last year. But even then, Rita had put tomato sauce on everything.

Natalie followed her grandmother into the house. "Vindaloo is a type of Indian curry and it's really delicious. You should give it a try, Gran."

Rita shuddered. "No thanks. What's wrong with some good old Aussie tucker? Give me a meat pie with tomato sauce and mushy peas any day."

"How about a pizza then?" suggested Natalie.

"Yeah, all right, I can cope with that."

Rita went around switching on the lights and drawing the curtains as Natalie called the pizza delivery service and put the order through. Then she returned to the kitchen, where her grandmother was making a cup of tea. She paused in the doorway as she suddenly saw something on the counter.

It was the card from the post this morning—the one she had thrown in the bin. Her grandmother must have fished it out again.

"Why don't you open it?" Rita said gently.

Natalie's mouth tightened. "You should have left it in the bin."

"Why don't you give him a chance? You don't even know what he has to say." Rita pushed the card towards Natalie. "Just open it and read it."

"I'm not interested in anything he has to say."

Rita sighed. "If I didn't know you better, Natalie, I'd think you were scared."

"Scared?"

"Why else wouldn't you want to at least see what he says? What are you afraid of?"

"I'm *not* afraid! I just don't want to have anything to do with him! I'm not some pathetic groupie dazzled by the stupid rock star thing!" Natalie realised that she was yelling and took a deep breath. "Sorry, Gran. I didn't mean to shout."

Rita sighed again. "I just think you should keep an open mind. He's been trying so hard and for so long now... why don't you just give him a chance? Maybe once you get to know him…" She took a step forwards and said gently, "After all, I'm not going to be around forever. It's important that you don't cut yourself off. You need other family. He *is* your fa—"

"He's not my *anything*! He's nothing to me!"

Natalie snatched up the card and tossed it into the bin again. Then she whirled and ran from the room.

CHAPTER FIVE

Natalie looked up from her notes and smiled at Craig and Sara across the conference table. "So are you planning a bridal shower? They're not so common here in Australia, but I know it's a really popular American tradition."

Sara hesitated. "Well... Ellie was really keen on one, but to be honest, I don't want to bother with it. For one thing, with half the family and guests overseas, we're not really doing gifts the traditional way. Plus I never liked the idea of sitting there opening all those presents—"

"Are blokes allowed to come to the shower?" asked Craig with a grin. "Or are you girls all going to be screaming over the sexy fireman stripper?"

"I think you're thinking of a hen night, Craig, not a bridal shower," said Natalie with a laugh.

"Yes, nothing wild in a bridal shower. But it *is* usually girls only," said Sara. "It's usually like a tea party or an afternoon at the spa with facials and make-up lessons..."

Craig made a face. "Then I vote that we jack it and let's just all go down to the pub—girls and blokes together. Much more fun."

"Yeah, I think I would prefer that too," Sara agreed.

Natalie nodded and made a note on her pad. "Okay. And I know you've decided you want the ceremony on the beach, right by the water—were you thinking of a more formal setup with an aisle and altar?"

Sara looked thoughtful. "Not formal exactly... but I love the look of those wedding canopies I've seen in photos, with the couple standing underneath. Do you think it would be hard to rig up something like that?"

"No, I should be able to organise that pretty easily. I could source some rustic bamboo poles and drape some white gauze fabric on top." Natalie turned her laptop around and showed Craig and Sara a couple of images on the screen. "I did some research last night and came up with these options that I could easily reproduce here."

"Oh, I love that!" said Sara, leaning forwards excitedly to look at a picture of a wedding arbour decorated with roses and glittering pink hearts.

"I'm not getting married underneath some

poncey pink archway," said Craig with a look of mock horror on his face

"Aw, come on, Craig," Sara said. "It's gorgeous! Look at the way the colours blend together and—"

Craig shook his head firmly. "No. No bloody way."

Sara pouted prettily. "Fine. What about this one then? I like this white and lavender one as well."

Craig eyed the screen sceptically. "I could cope with that, I guess."

"Are you planning to wear heels?" Natalie asked Sara. "If you want my advice, you're best to stick to sandals or even wedges if you really need a bit of height. Heels will keep sinking into the sand and be a nightmare to walk in. But if you really want to wear heels, I can arrange to have a wooden walkway buried under the sand. It will still look like a sandy beach, but it'll make it possible for you be able to walk with heels down the aisle to the ceremony area."

"No, that's okay—I'll just find some pretty sandals to go with my wedding gown."

"Why not go barefoot?" asked Craig. "We said this isn't a super formal wedding. I know I'm wearing a linen suit, but I can tell you most Aussie blokes are just going to come in a shirt and smart trousers. Why not just forget about shoes altogether?"

"Yes, I think barefoot beach weddings are gorgeous," said Natalie enthusiastically.

Sara smiled. "Okay! We'll both be barefoot then. But I'd still like to have some kind of aisle to walk down."

"No worries, I can still create one in the sand and decorate the edges to mark it. I think using natural themed decor will look the best. Things like shells or starfish or little wooden seahorses like this..." Natalie reached into her folder and pulled out a little carved wooden seahorse, no bigger than her palm.

"That's beautiful! Where did you find that?" asked Sara, reaching out to take it.

Natalie smiled. "A local artist makes these out of driftwood. His name is Ru. He's a Samoan fisherman—but he's a really talented artist as well."

"Oh, I know Ru!" said Sara excitedly. "He was one of the first people I met when I arrived in Australia. In fact, he gave me directions to the beach on the first day." She glanced at Craig and gave him a whimsical smile "You might say he helped get us together. I was totally lost and if he hadn't directed me, maybe I wouldn't have gotten to the beach in time to find that lost Beagle... and then I would have never come to the animal hospital... and never met you..."

Craig reached out and caught Sara's hand. "I'm sure we would have still met somehow. A place the size of Summer Beach—I would have been sure to notice you around and I would have made damned sure that I got to know you." He grinned. "But I'm glad Ru speeded things up."

Natalie felt slightly embarrassed as she watched Sara and Craig smile into each other's eyes. She felt like an intruder in a private moment. And she also felt slightly wistful. They were so in love—it was there in the way they kept glancing at each other and found ways to brush each other's hands, exchange looks and smiles... Would she ever get the chance to feel this kind of special closeness with someone too?

It was true that she had always shied away from romantic attachments and stamped out the chance of anything more developing whenever a man had shown interest. But even if she were to change her attitude, who could she meet? She was unlikely to move far from Summer Beach and how was she supposed to find her special someone when she was stuck in this little corner of Australia?

Then she looked at Craig and Sara again, and remembered that Sara was American. She had lived eight thousand miles on the other side of the ocean and yet still, she and Craig had found each other. *Who's to know who I might meet?* Natalie thought. Then for some reason, her mind flashed back to yesterday morning and the encounter with that sexy resort guest, Ben. She felt a faint blush come to her cheeks and hurriedly looked down, busying herself shuffling some papers.

Sara held up the wooden seahorse. "I love this. And I love the special meaning with the role Ru played, to have him be part of the wedding in some way. He's on our guest list, of course, but to have something made by him would be even more special. I'd like to order a whole batch from him and make it a theme for the wedding, what do you think? We could use these in the decorations and to anchor the place-cards at the reception—and maybe give them away at the end of the evening, as little mementos for our guests. It would be really nice way to support Ru and give back to the local community too."

"Yeah, ripper idea," said Craig.

"Okay, I'll contact Ru and get it all sorted," Natalie said. "And I'll finalise the menu with Jean-Pierre, the Head Resort Chef, and get back to you about the cake. I've also organised a meeting for you guys with the photographer tomorrow, to discuss the style of shots you'd like."

"Just to let you know, Natalie," said Craig quickly. "There will probably be extra photographers and film crew on the day. And maybe coming along to some of these prep sessions. I've done a deal with the studio producing my TV show and they're filming a special feature on the wedding."

Natalie raised her eyebrows. She noticed that Sara hadn't said anything. In fact, the other girl looked slightly uncomfortable.

"Oh-kay," Natalie said. "That shouldn't be an issue, as long as they stay in the background. But I assume that you'd like your own photos too and wouldn't just rely on the ones from the paparazzi?"

"Yes, especially as they seem to specialise in getting pictures of my butt looking huge," muttered Sara.

Natalie gave her a sympathetic smile, then glanced at her notepad again. "Okay... I think we've covered everything for now. I need the final guest list from you by tomorrow, and any particular requirements such as disabled access or special diets... oh, wait—the music. We haven't talked about the music yet. Have you—"

"I've got that all sorted," said Craig with a smile. "A good friend of mine is coming to the wedding and he's offered to provide the music. He'll sort out a backing band."

"Is he a professional musician?" asked Natalie sceptically.

Craig grinned. "Oh, *yeah*..."

"You never told me about this friend?" said Sara with a puzzled frown.

"Well, we met when I was in the U.S. doing my fellowship in Veterinary Neurology. He's not a vet— but he was at the same college. He used to sing in one of the student bands and I went to watch them one night; we had a couple of beers together afterwards and really hit it off. We haven't seen each other much since I came back to Oz. We caught up when I went back to the States a few times, but this will be his first trip to Australia."

"And he's a musician?"

Craig nodded. "He's not that well known yet here in Australia, but his career's really taking off in the States. He's been signed up by one of the biggest labels and his tour last year sold out in a week. You'll love his music—he's got the most amazing voice." He glanced at his watch. "I asked him to come and join us here this morning, so you could both meet him. I thought he'd be here by now, actually. I wonder what's keeping him—"

As if on cue, a knock sounded at the conference room door, then it swung open. Natalie froze as a tall, handsome young man stepped into the room. He was dressed in a light blue, checked shirt and black jeans, rather than the board shorts that she had last seen him in, and his wavy dark hair was not wet and plastered against his brow, but she recognised him instantly.

It was the man she had rescued yesterday morning.

Craig stood up and went towards his friend, and the two men exchanged a hearty handshake. Then Craig turned back to Sara and Natalie and said with a grin:

"Girls, I'd like you to meet Ben Falco—our resident rock star."

CHAPTER SIX

Natalie felt the blood roaring in her ears. She stared at the man across the room. *Ben? Ben was a rocker?* He looked around and their eyes met, and Natalie felt that tug of attraction again, stronger than anything she had ever experienced. But it didn't fill her with excitement this time. It filled her with fear.

Sara stood up. "Ben Falco? Oh my God, I know you! My cousin, Ellie, loves your music. She'll go nuts when she finds out you're going to be at the wedding." She turned to Craig and laughed. "Forget the paparazzi—they're not going to worry about us when they find out that a rock superstar like Ben's going to be at the wedding."

Ben came over to the conference table, holding up his hands with palms out. "Please. Let's just drop the rock star thing. I'm just here as a good friend and I happen to be able to sing, so I thought I'd play my part by providing some music for the night."

"And can he bloody well sing," said Craig, nodding enthusiastically.

"I can relate to wanting to keep out of the media spotlight," said Sara.

Ben sighed. "Yeah, I don't know how much longer I'll be able to stay incognito. The resort has been great about helping me keep a low profile. I know the paparazzi followed me from the States over to Sydney, but I think I shook them off between the airport and here." He looked at Craig. "Man, I can't tell you how happy I am to be in a place like Summer Beach where nobody knows me and there aren't cameras everywhere. And I have to say, so far, the bit I've seen of Australia is pretty awesome."

"Summer Beach is special," said Sara with a smile. "I mean, I know it looks like any other sleepy little seaside town on the coast, but there's something about this place…" She turned to Natalie. "Don't you agree, Natalie? I think you're so lucky to have lived here all your life."

They all turned to look at her. Natalie realised that she was the only person still sitting. She stood up hastily.

"Er… yes," she said. She saw that Craig and Sara were looking at her expectantly and she hastily offered her hand to Ben. "Hi."

He took it in his firm grasp and she felt that familiar prickle of awareness. Quickly she pulled her hand away from him and sat down again, shuffling some papers unnecessarily.

Ben looked at her quizzically, then turned back to Craig and Sara. "Actually, Natalie and I met yesterday. She rescued me from a jellyfish attack and took me to the hospital."

"Crikey, you're not serious, mate?" said Craig.

Ben gave a wry smile. "I wish I wasn't. You should see what my leg looked like. But it's a lot better today, all thanks to Natalie."

"It was nothing," murmured Natalie. She refused to meet his eyes.

Ben gave her another funny look, then turned away as Craig began talking about the wedding music again. Natalie fiddled with her pen and notepad, although she didn't write anything. It was just as well that Craig and Sara were doing most of the talking, because her brain seemed to have frozen like a crashing computer. She was aware of a mix of emotions washing over her: horror and dismay mixed with bitter disappointment

"Natalie?"

She jumped. She realised suddenly that the room was empty now except for her and Ben. The door was open and she could see Craig and Sara standing in the hallway outside, talking to the resort chef. They must have finished the music discussions for now. She had completely missed the conversation. She hoped that it hadn't been too obvious.

"I didn't realise you were the Event Coordinator when you said you worked for the resort," said Ben with a smile.

Natalie didn't return his smile. "Yes, I've only just started."

"I wanted to say thank you again for yesterday."

"There's no need," she said stiffly.

"I'm having lunch with Craig and Sara and then they're showing me around Summer Beach a bit, but I'm really looking forward to our dinner tonight. You still okay for seven o'clock?"

"Actually..." Natalie stood up and began to gather her things from the table. "I'm sorry, but I can't make it after all."

Ben frowned. "Okay… How about tomorrow night then?"

"Tomorrow night's not good either," said Natalie shortly.

She shut her laptop and slid it into its case, then shouldered her handbag and picked up the folder in her arms.

"Wait… Are you saying that you can't have dinner with me at all?"

Natalie met his gaze, then looked quickly away. "I'm sorry. I just don't think it would be appropriate."

"What do you mean?" asked Ben, frowning. "You're just helping to organise my friend's wedding. I don't understand… Yesterday you were fine with it. What's changed?"

Natalie glanced at him again and the confusion in his eyes tugged at her heartstrings. She hesitated. Then she remembered again who he was. *What* he was.

"I just… I'm sorry, I just don't think it's a good idea. Now, if you'll excuse me, I… I've got another meeting to go to."

She turned and hurried from the room, leaving him staring after her.

CHAPTER SEVEN

Sara laughed as she watched her Beagle, Coco, dance excitedly around the front door.

"Okay, girl. Just a minute—let me put your leash on..."

She bent down and clipped a leash onto the dog's collar, then paused to lace up her sneakers, before grabbing her keys and opening the front door. She was looking forward to the walk and the chance to get some fresh air; to forget about things for a bit.

It had been a stressful week, what with trying to make sure she had covered things at her new job before she went on leave and keeping on top of preparations for the wedding. And now her parents and some of her family were arriving from the States the day after tomorrow. They would be staying at the resort, which had more than enough amenities to entertain them, but still, Sara felt like she had to clear the decks before they arrived so that she could spend time with them without worrying.

But for now, it was just nice to spend an hour down on the beach with Coco. Walking her little Beagle always lifted her spirits and helped to soothe her frayed nerves. There was something about the way dogs seemed to live in the moment—the way they sniffed every bush and rock as if they had never seen it before, ran with such joyous abandon, and took such pleasure in the simplest things—that made you smile and feel better about everything. Only another dog lover could really understand, but animal therapy was one of the best medicines.

Sara locked the front door behind her and started down the road, with Coco pulling eagerly at the end of her leash. She had moved in with Craig a few months ago, and she was reminded every day of what a fantastic location his house was in: perched high up on the cliffs overlooking Summer Beach, with a view from the living room and back terrace out over the Pacific Ocean. And even more conveniently, there was a small sign a few yards down the road from Craig's front door which marked the start of a trail leading down through the bush to the beach below. This was usually the route she took when she walked Coco and her little hound turned automatically in that direction.

But before they had gone a few steps, Sara was surprised to hear her name being called. She turned to see a man and woman getting out of a car that was parked in the cul-de-sac. She eyed them warily as they approached her. The man was holding a TV camera with a wide lens and microphone attached. The woman next to him looked vaguely familiar—Sara thought she might have seen her before at the animal hospital when there was filming for Craig's TV show.

"Hi Sara, I'm Jenn. I'm the assistant producer for *Aussie Beach Vet*. I don't think we've been properly introduced." The girl held a hand out.

Sara shook it absently, her gaze still on the TV camera. "No, I don't think we have. I'm sorry—I don't understand why you're here?"

"Oh, well, Craig told us that you were on board with the special wedding feature," Jenn said excitedly. "So we thought we'd start getting footage right away. You want the viewers to feel like they were with you every step of the way, which means we'd like to cover some of the lead-up to the actual day."

"Yes, but I'm not doing anything related to the wedding right now," Sara said.

Jenn waved her hand dismissively. "Oh, it doesn't matter. Of course, the main things we'll be shooting will be things like your hair consult and dress fittings and stuff like that, but we wanted to get some footage of daily life too. You, know, all the things a bride does in the run-up to her big day."

"Well..." Sara said doubtfully. "I'm just walking my dog."

Jenn looked her up and down, taking in the tank top, shorts, and trainers. "You look like you're heading for a good workout. Are you worried about fitting into your dress? Trying to lose that last bit of weight, perhaps?"

"No!" snapped Sara. She took a deep breath, then said in a calmer voice, "No, I'm not trying to lose weight. I fit into my dress fine. This is just my usual walk."

Jenn raised her eyebrows. "There's nothing to be ashamed of, you know. Lots of brides feel like they need to lose some serious weight and really work on their figures before their wedding. It's something a lot of our viewers can relate to."

"Well, that's not what I'm doing!" said Sara shortly. "I'm sorry if it's not such good TV fodder, but I'm not worried about my figure for the wedding!"

Jenn's eyebrows climbed even higher and Sara flushed. Even without the other woman's scepticism, she knew that what she had said was untrue. She *was* worried about her figure. She *always* worried about her figure. And with this wedding, every one of her usual worries seemed to have doubled. She glanced irritably at the cameraman. And now, on top of all that, she felt like there were additional magnifying glasses on every inch of her body.

"We'd just like to come along and film a bit of you walking your dog," Jenn said soothingly. "It would make a nice break in between the other scenes of wedding prep, in the final programme, and shots of the beach are always good. We'll stay out of your way," she promised.

Sara couldn't think of any way to refuse without seeming churlish. She shrugged, then turned and led Coco to the beginning of the track. She started down the trail, determined to act like she didn't have a film crew following her. It was hard, though, as she could hear their footsteps clattering on the trail behind her. And she couldn't help her mind going back to what Jenn had just said. *Why had she made that comment? Does she think that I look fat? Is that how I'm looking on camera now? Is the guy filming me already? Oh God, why did I decide to wear these shorts today? They're old and baggy and so unflattering...*

Sara shook her head in annoyance. She chose these shorts because they were the most comfortable. And she hadn't cared how she looked because she hadn't been expecting to have cameras on her while she was just walking her dog!

They reached the beach and Sara unclipped Coco from the leash so that the Beagle could have run free. She watched as the dog raced across the sand, barking with joy and chasing some seagulls in the distance. She felt her mood lighten and her irritation fade away. She took a deep breath and pushed away the thought of the two people behind her. She was here to enjoy a walk with her dog and she was not going to let them spoil it for her.

Instead, she concentrated on the beautiful scene in front of her: the waves washing up on the beach, the sun making its slow way down the horizon, and the sand reflecting the soft golden flow of the afternoon. Coco came running back, her tongue lolling out and her eyes bright with excitement. Sara laughed, her mood lifting even more. Coco ran around her and barked expectantly.

"All right," Sara said as she withdrew a tennis ball from her pocket. She lobbed it across the beach and watched her dog take off after it, neck outstretched, paws pounding the sand. In a minute, Coco was back, dropping the ball at Sara's feet. Sara smiled and patted the Beagle's head, then reached down to pick up the ball. As she straightened, she realised that Jenn and the cameraman had closed the gap and were right behind her. In fact, from the corner of her eye, she could see the cameraman training the lens right on her butt!

Sara whirled to face them. "Can you guys back off a bit?" she asked irritably.

Before they could reply, she turned and marched off again, walking faster to try and get away from her followers. Then she noticed three other figures in the distance. As they got closer, she saw that it was her cousin, Ellie, together with a young boy and a huge chocolate Labrador.

Of course, it had to be Will and Milo, she thought with a smile. Ellie hardly ever came down to the beach without her young friend and his faithful dog. They had seen her too: Ellie waved and Milo began to wag his tail excitedly. He launched himself forwards, galloping across the beach towards them.

"*Oomph!*" Sara staggered back as the Labrador jumped up and flung himself onto her chest. He was wriggling with excitement, trying to lick her. Then she realised that he was moving other parts of his body. *Oh no.* Milo was humping her enthusiastically and everything was being caught on camera.

"Milo! Get off me!" she admonished, trying to push the chocolate Lab down.

"Milo! Down! Bad boy!" Will shouted as he ran up and grabbed his dog's collar.

Ellie arrived too, trying to hide a grin.

"It's not funny," Sara spluttered, still trying to push the Labrador off her. Finally, she managed to disengage herself.

"Sorry, but it was a pretty funny, right?" guffawed Ellie.

"Yeah, and I'm sure it'll make brilliant prime time viewing," muttered Sara darkly, glancing across at Jenn and the cameramen a few feet behind her

Ellie followed Sara's gaze. "Who are they?"

"The film crew for the special wedding feature," said Sara with a sigh. "They turned up on my doorstep and insisted on following me while I walked Coco. But they're really getting on my nerves."

A volley of barking made them both turn around. Milo had bounded over to Coco and was now prancing around the Beagle, bowing and trying to invite her to play. But the smaller dog was backing away, her tail down and her eyes uncertain. The two dogs had met several times since Coco had cleared quarantine after coming from the U.S. and they had even been out on several "play dates". But Sara's gentle Beagle had never quite taken to the boisterous Labrador. The problem was, they had completely different doggie personalities—Coco's soft, docile temperament the very opposite of Milo's mischievous exuberance—and this wasn't going to change any time soon.

Milo barked again in frustration and then— obviously deciding to take matters into his paws— launched himself onto the Beagle and rolled her over, wagging his tail excitedly as he tried to chew on her ears. Coco squealed and wriggled out from under him, scampering back to Sara and hiding behind her legs.

Sara felt a flare of irritation. She didn't normally mind Milo's antics too much, but today, something snapped.

"You really need to do something about Milo,

Will! He's becoming a total nuisance. He can't just go barging up to everyone and jumping all over them!"

"I... I'm sorry," said Will, hanging his head. The colour left his small, freckled face. "Milo's just really friendly..."

"Well, not everyone needs his 'friendliness' thrust into their faces," Sara snapped.

"Hey..." Ellie, put a protective arm around Will's shoulders and frowned at Sara. "Will's trying. He's started taking Milo to dog training classes every week. But Milo is still really young and Labradors are just really energetic, friendly dogs. You have to remember, Coco is a lot older... plus, she's got a different personality."

"Oh, and you're suddenly an expert on dogs now, are you? I thought you didn't even like them," said Sara.

Ellie started to retort, then caught herself. She turned to Will and pointed to the tennis ball lying in the sand a few feet away from them.

"Will—why don't you play that game where you throw the ball and race with the dogs to see who catches it first?"

"Okay!" said Will eagerly, running to grab the ball.

Milo instantly ran over to the boy, barking excitedly. Will threw the ball and the two dogs took off after it, with the boy following.

As soon as he was out of earshot, Ellie turned

back to Sara and said, "Okay, coz, what's going on? You know it was unfair of you to lay into Will like that just now. He's only a kid. And yeah, I didn't used to like dogs, but I've changed my mind. Everyone is entitled to do that. And I'm educating myself about them—what's wrong with that?"

Sara felt a wave of shame wash over her. She looked down. "Sorry. I don't know what's come over me. I just..."

She glanced behind her. She could see Jenn and the cameraman a few yards away. They had stopped filming and had their heads together, watching the playback on his camera.

Sara turned back to Ellie and took a deep breath. "You're right, I shouldn't have taken out my bad mood out on Will." She sighed. "I don't know... I just... I'm feeling so stressed out with this wedding. And having the film crew following my every move doesn't help. I mean, God knows what they're filming and what I look like—"

"You've gotta relax," said Ellie impatiently. "Stop worrying about what you look like! Everyone else thinks you look gorgeous." She took a step closer and laid a gentle hand on Sara's arm. "Look, I know having the camera around is bringing back bad memories of everything that happened back in L.A. with Jeff—but you've got to try and put that behind you."

"Easy for you to say," muttered Sara.

"Well, if you feel that strongly about it, you

should tell Craig that you've changed your mind about having them do the feature."

"I can't do that now! I've already agreed to do it. And they've already made a big press announcement about it and about us donating the money to charity. Everyone is really excited and loves the idea—and it's given Craig's public profile a huge boost since the news came out yesterday."

Ellie shrugged. "Well, in that case... I guess you're going to have to learn to deal with it. You know that saying 'No one can make you feel inferior without your permission'—I think it was Eleanor Roosevelt who said that?"

Sara sighed. "You're right." She looked up as Will rejoined them with two happy, panting dogs right behind him. Coco looked a bit more relaxed now and she didn't seem to mind Milo trotting along beside her.

"Will... I'm sorry I snapped at you just now," Sara said, putting a hand on the boy's thin shoulder. "I was in a bad mood about something else, but I shouldn't have taken it out on you."

Will grinned. "It's okay. My mum gets maggoty too sometimes."

"How *is* your mother?" asked Sara. She remembered that Will's mother suffered from depression and things had been very difficult since his parents had separated last year. She felt another stab of guilt at her sharp words to the boy.

"She's okay," said Will. "She's going out of the

house more now and she even came to my school fair last week." He grinned and added in a rush, his words tumbling over each other, "Ellie came and got her from the house and stayed with her the whole time—and Mum said she really enjoyed it and she wouldn't have come if it hadn't been for Ellie but now she thinks she's going to come to my next one."

Ellie looked a bit embarrassed. "It was nothing," she said, reaching down to rub Milo's ears.

Will suddenly noticed the cameraman. "Are they filming us?"

Sara glanced back over her shoulder, then said ruefully, "Yes. They're doing a special wedding feature for Craig's TV show."

"Oh, beauty! Milo's going to be on TV!" cried Will, dancing around.

Milo perked up on hearing his name and bounced around the boy, barking loudly. Will whooped and skipped, rousing Milo even more. The chocolate Lab started running around in circles, beside himself with excitement. He rushed up to Coco and jumped on her, trying to hump her head.

"Milo!" Sara cried.

"Oy! Milo—get off!" shouted Will, running forwards to grab the Lab's collar. He hauled Milo off Coco. The Beagle shook herself and scooted back to Sara's side.

"Sorry..." said Will with a sheepish grin. "He's just started doing that. He keeps doing it at home to Mum's favourite cushion as well. It really annoys her."

"Isn't he fixed?" asked Sara in exasperation. "Why is he still doing this?"

"Humping isn't always about sex," said Ellie quickly. "It can just be an over-excitement thing, especially with young dogs. And before you think I'm trying to be some dog expert, Dan told me that."

"Well, if he *has* to do it, I'd prefer he did it to a cushion and not to Coco," said Sara peevishly. She reached down and patted her dog. "Anyway, I think we'd better be heading back—enough excitement for one day." She turned away, then turned back. "Oh, Ellie—do you want to come over tonight? We've invited Ben over for a barbecue. He was supposed to have dinner with someone, I think, but they've cancelled on him and Craig doesn't want him to be sitting alone at the resort."

"You bet," said Ellie enthusiastically. "Who'd say no to dinner with Ben Falco? Oh my God, I still can't believe he's going to sing at the wedding!"

"Who's Ben Falco?" asked Will.

"He's a rock star. He's pretty famous in the United States," Ellie explained. "And he's come for Sara and Craig's wedding."

"Wow!" Will's eyes were wide. "Can I get to meet him?"

"I'm sure you'll see him at the wedding," said Sara kindly. "If you like, you can come to the rehearsal as well and meet him there first."

"Oh, can I?" Will gave a little hop. "Can Milo

come too?"

Sara looked at the Labrador askance. "Well... okay, I guess. Coco's going to be at the rehearsal because she's the 'ring bearer'—so I suppose another dog won't matter."

"Coco's going to be the ring bearer?" Ellie smirked.

Sara gave her cousin a mock glare. "Don't laugh. Lots of people do it. There are even special ring-bearer pillows for dogs to wear. And I got this gorgeous satin and lace collar for Coco. She'll look so cute."

"Can Milo be a ring bearer too?" Will asked eagerly. "Then he can wear a tuxedo collar! I've seen these doggie bow ties—I've saved up my pocket money! I can get one for Milo!"

Sara hesitated. Much as she liked Milo, the thought of the unruly Labrador at her wedding made her heart sink. But looking down at the boy's hopeful face, she couldn't bear the thought of disappointing him.

"Well, there's usually only one ring bearer, you see..." she said to Will.

"That's okay! Milo can just walk next to Coco when she's carrying the ring down the aisle. Sort of like the ring bearer's bodyguard—yeah?"

"Well, I..." Sara hesitated, then smiled at him. "Okay. Milo can be Assistant Ring Bearer at the wedding."

"WOOHOO!" Will jumped up, punching the air.

"Did you hear that, Milo? You're going to be Assistant Ring Bearer! Yay! Yay! Hurray!" He skipped away down the beach, laughing and cheering, whilst Milo raced after him, barking excitedly.

Ellie gave Sara's arm a squeeze. "Thanks. That was a really nice thing to do. You didn't have to, but you really made his day."

Sara gave a rueful smile as she watched Milo run loops around the boy. "I just hope I don't regret it."

CHAPTER EIGHT

"Ow!" Natalie yanked her hand back and sucked her thumb. She had just narrowly missed crushing it between two bamboo poles. She lowered the pole she was holding back to the sand and sighed. It had looked so easy when she was at the bamboo suppliers. They had assured her that these DIY pre-constructed wedding canopy kits would be simple to set up and ideal for her situation.

"If you can put together an IKEA cabinet, you can do this," the owner had told her cheerfully.

So Natalie had eagerly purchased the kit and returned to the resort. She did have to ask one of the resort porters to help her lug it from her car to the beach, but she had been convinced that once she was left on her own and had a bit of time to study the instructions, she would have the structure erected in no time.

That was nearly an hour ago and she didn't seem to have progressed much further beyond getting the four vertical poles of the canopy anchored upright in the sand. Now she was trying to get one of the crossbars into place, but she just couldn't wedge it into the pre-cut slots on the vertical poles. Perhaps it would help if she was a bit taller—trying to stand on your tiptoes in the sand and balance, whilst wedging a two-metre long bamboo pole securely into a narrow opening, was not the easiest feat.

"Need some help?"

Natalie dropped the pole and spun around. Ben stood behind her, his hand in his pockets, a smile on his face. He was back in his board shorts again and she couldn't help noticing the way the late afternoon sun played across the defined muscles of his chest and shoulders, and brought out the golden tan to his skin. He looked like he had been walking along the beach—his bare feet were caked with sand and his dark hair tousled—and he must have come a fair way. Natalie had purposely chosen this secluded spot farther down from the popular area in front of main resort buildings and the pool; she didn't think many of the guests would wander this far.

She realised that Ben was still waiting for her to answer. She hesitated. She hadn't seen him since that meeting in the conference room yesterday morning and had been trying not to think about him since. Her conscience *had* pricked her last night, though, when she had suddenly had a vision of him sitting by himself over some lonely dinner in one of the resort restaurants. Then she had given herself a mental shake. What was she thinking? Of course he wouldn't have been alone. This was Ben Falco! If he hadn't been with Craig and Sara, she was sure there would have been no end of female offers to keep him company. *Not that it's any of my business, of course*, she thought hastily.

But here and now, there was no good reason for her to refuse his help and, in any case, she *did* need to get this canopy up. It seemed stupid not to take up his offer.

"Thanks, yes, that would be great..." she said grudgingly.

Ben came forwards and lifted the bamboo pole easily from the sand, then reached up and held it across two of the vertical poles. With his height, getting it into the right position was easy, and in a moment he had slotted it into place and clicked it in.

"Want to pass me the matching crossbar for the other side?" He held his hand out to her.

"Um... Yes, of course..." Natalie snapped out of her reverie and scrambled to pull the other crossbar from the canvas bag.

As she passed it over to Ben, their fingers brushed and she felt that thrill of awareness shoot up her arm again. If Ben felt anything, however, he showed no sign of it. He quickly assembled the crossbar on the other side of the canopy, then—working together—they put up the remaining sections and pieces.

"Looks great," said Ben with an approving nod as they stood back to look at their handiwork.

Natalie nodded, feeling a sense of satisfaction. Even without drapes and decorations, the canopy already looked elegant and romantic, with the beach and ocean forming a spectacular backdrop. The light from the setting sun played over the graceful lines of the criss-crossing bamboo poles. Once decorated with organza, ribbons, and flowers, it would look absolutely stunning.

She glanced at Ben, then said stiffly, "Thanks for your help. I think I would have been struggling here until midnight if you hadn't come along."

Ben smiled at her. "Anytime."

Natalie felt her stomach flip over at that smile. "I... I've got to get back," she said quickly, picking up the empty canvas bag and turning towards the main resort building.

"I'll walk you back," said Ben, falling into step beside her.

Natalie felt a mixture of emotions wash over her. She knew she had to keep away from Ben—he was bad news—and yet she couldn't help feeling a treacherous thrill of pleasure at the thought of a bit more time with him.

They said nothing as they walked slowly back

towards the main buildings. The beach was deserted now as the sun had set and darkness was falling. Most people had gone in to shower and change for dinner. Stars were beginning to twinkle in the sky, and behind them the crashing of the waves seemed to have muted and faded to a hushed murmur.

"Wow. The sky really *is* different here. All the stars seem to be upside down," said Ben.

He had slowed to a standstill and was looking up at the sky, tilting his head one way and the other. Natalie paused reluctantly beside him.

Ben pointed up at the sky. "There's Orion's Belt. Do you guys have the same names for the constellations?"

Natalie hesitated. There was something intimate about standing here next to him, looking up at the stars together. She didn't want to prolong the moment, but she felt like she had no choice. It would have been too rude to just keep walking and leave him behind. And now that he had asked a direct question, she could hardly avoid talking either.

"Actually, the Aboriginals looked at the stars differently," she said. "They often looked at the dark patches between the stars rather than at the stars themselves. For example, what we see as the Milky Way, they see as a giant emu, with the dark patches between the stars making up its body."

"I like that," said Ben with a smile. "Focusing on

the spaces in between. Kind of like reading between the lines or when the real message is in the things left unsaid."

"I suppose you're going to turn that into song lyrics for your next No. 1 hit or something," said Natalie sarcastically.

Ben looked at her. "I hadn't thought about it, but now that you mention it, yes, they would make beautiful lyrics," he said evenly.

Natalie flushed and turned quickly towards the steps that led up from the beach to the pool area. In her haste, she stumbled and tripped over the first step.

"Careful!" Ben grabbed her, stopping her just in time from face-planting on the steps. He eased her back upright.

"Th-thanks," Natalie said, very aware that Ben still hadn't let go of her arm. She could feel his fingers on the bare skin of her forearms, burning against her skin. "I'm okay now." She pulled away.

"I'll walk you to your car," said Ben.

"No, there's no need," said Natalie quickly. "Thanks again for your help."

She turned quickly and hurried away, forcing herself not to look back although she could feel his gaze following her out of sight.

Natalie found it hard to keep her mind on her work the next day. She was annoyed with herself because she found that her thoughts kept returning to one sexy American rock star... the way he had looked, standing on the beach with his dark hair tousled by the sea breeze and the soft glow of the setting sun playing across his handsome features... She could still vividly remember the feel of his fingers on the bare skin of her arm and the deep heather-grey of his eyes as he gazed down at her.

Stop thinking about him, she admonished herself as she shut down her computer for the day and tidied her desk. Her distracted state had already caused her to make several mistakes today, which meant that she had had to redo a number of things and ended up staying late. It was nearly seven already. She had phoned her grandmother earlier to let her know about the delay, but she knew that Rita would begin to worry if she stayed much later.

She closed her office door and turned around, then started as she nearly bumped into Craig.

"Natalie—I'm so pleased I caught you!" he said. "I thought you might have left already, but I reckoned I'd give it a try."

"What's the matter?" said Natalie. "Is it the flowers for the wedding? Because tell Sara don't worry about that—it will all be sorted by tomorrow and then you and she can—"

"No, no, it's nothing to do with the wedding," said Craig. "Are you free tonight?"

"Uh... yeah. I was just heading home, actually."

"Can you could do me a favour?"

"Sure." Natalie looked at him curiously.

"See, I was supposed to spend the evening with Ben, but something's come up at the clinic and I'll need to head back there now. I'll probably be there till late. And Sara's gone down to Sydney Airport with Ellie to pick up their parents. I hate the thought of Ben spending the whole evening alone. He doesn't know anyone else here in Summer Beach. Then I thought of you. Do you think you could sort of... 'look after' Ben for me this evening? We've just had a snack together so you don't have to have some big dinner if you don't want. Maybe the two of you could have a drink or something?"

Craig looked at Natalie earnestly. "I know this isn't part of your official duties for the wedding, but this would mean a lot to me. And I suppose you could look on Ben as the 'music' for the wedding. Maybe you could see it as a trade for the time you would have spent researching bands or sorting out a DJ? What do you say?"

"I..." Natalie stared at him, not knowing how to answer. The last thing she wanted to do was spend the evening with Ben, but how could she refuse now? She cursed herself for telling Craig so quickly that she was free that evening. She could have simply pretended that she had another engagement and got out of it.

"Of course, we'd be happy to pay for your time," added Craig, seeing her hesitation.

"No, it's not the money..." said Natalie. "You and

Sara have been more than generous with what you're paying me already."

"Then you're okay with it?" said Craig eagerly.

Natalie hesitated again, then sighed. "I'll need to ring my grandmother first and check with her."

Craig nodded. "No worries, I'll wait for you in the lobby."

When he was gone, Natalie rang her grandmother, hoping that the latter would suddenly have some reason for needing her home urgently. But Rita sounded delighted with the idea, especially when she heard that Natalie would be spending the evening with Ben.

"You go and have some fun—don't worry about me," she said. "Good for you to go out for a change. You don't spent enough time with other young people. Is this that spunky young man you rescued the other morning?"

"Who says he's spunky?"

"Ah, just something I picked up from what you said..." Natalie could hear the smile in her grandmother's voice.

"Yeah, it is him, Gran, but it's just a work thing really. I'm only doing it to help Craig out because I'm their wedding coordinator and I suppose you could say this is part of the wedding duties in a way. Ben is going be providing the music so it's really no different to me meeting up with the photographer or the florist..." Natalie trailed off as she realised that she was protesting a bit too much.

"I'm sure it is." Rita Walker's voice sounded amused. "Well, you have a lovely time, dear. And don't worry about rushing back for me. Stay out as late as you like!"

I certainly won't be taking Gran up on her offer, thought Natalie as she made her way out to the lobby. She was going to have this drink with Ben and get it over with as soon as possible. The last thing she wanted to do was to spend the whole evening in Ben Falco's company!

CHAPTER NINE

"Look... This is stupid. There's no need for you to do this," said Ben as soon as Craig had left them. "I'm perfectly capable of amusing myself for one evening. I don't need you to babysit me and go to all the trouble of—"

"It's no trouble," said Natalie woodenly. "I told Craig I'd be happy to do it."

Ben gave her a dry look, which said clearly that he didn't believe her words, but he made no further protest as Natalie suggested driving down to Newcastle to check out some of the bars and clubs there.

"We'll have to go in my car," she said. "Although I know it's probably not what you're used to as a rock superstar. If you want, we can get the hotel limousine to—"

"Hey, I was more than happy with your car the other day," said Ben with an easy smile. "Why should I have a problem now?"

Natalie nodded curtly and led the way out to the car park. They said nothing more as they pulled out of the resort car park and got onto the coastal freeway heading south, the music from the radio filling the awkward silence between them. Natalie couldn't help flashing back to that first morning she had met Ben, when they had sung together at the top of their voices, with the music going at full blast and the wind rushing in through the open windows. How different it all was now. *Why couldn't Ben have been just another resort guest?* she thought suddenly with bitter regret.

The drive wasn't long and they were soon pulling into the harbour city of Newcastle. As Australia's second oldest city and the next biggest metropolitan hub in New South Wales after Sydney, Newcastle was always well known as a surfer's Mecca due to its fantastic beaches. But it was also starting to gain a reputation for its vibrant arts and culture scene, and its host of cool bars and award-winning eateries.

They started at Honeysuckle Wharf and sipped cocktails at a couple of sophisticated bars with chic urban décor and water views, before moving on to the suburb of Cooks Hill, famous for its tree-lined streets and rows of Victorian terrace houses. The area also boasted a thriving night scene on Darby

Street, with several trendy pubs and bars, gourmet cafés, live music, and an easy-going, bohemian vibe.

Natalie felt her irritation growing, however, as she saw from Ben's expression that he didn't seem to be enjoying himself much. As they sat down at a table in an open-air bar on Darby Street, she scowled and said:

"I'm sorry these bars aren't up to your usual standards. I suppose they don't compare to the trendy places you're used to back in the U.S. with the rest of the cool crowd."

"No, these places are great," said Ben politely.

His refusal to complain irritated her even more.

"I suppose you're used to fancier places with designer décor and VIP lounges—"

"No, actually, the places I go to back home aren't that fancy at all," said Ben quietly. "And I'm not a huge drinker. I mean, I'll go out on a Friday or Saturday night with friends sometimes, but I don't go out boozing every night."

"Really?" Natalie raised her eyebrows. "Doesn't seem to go with the rock star image."

Ben gave her a teasing grin. "You mean the whole sex, drugs, and rock 'n' roll thing? That *is* just a cliché, you know."

"I thought clichés were created for a reason," said Natalie. "You don't need to hold yourself back on my account, you know. If you want to drink and... do stuff... Go ahead."

Ben's grin got even wider. "What sort of 'stuff' do you imagine I want to do?"

Natalie shrugged and looked away. On the other side of the bar, a small live band was playing up on the stage. The lead singer was a young guy with the sort of blond good looks that many women loved. He had just finished his song and took a bow to cheers and enthusiastic clapping. A couple of women squealed as they rushed over and grabbed him, giggling flirtatiously as they posed for a photo together.

"You must miss all that," Natalie said contemptuously, nodding in their direction. "I suppose back in the States, you'd get special treatment wherever you go and never have to wait for tables or anything at restaurants."

"No, actually, I don't miss it at all. And as for special treatment, yeah, that happens sometimes—but generally I like to keep a low profile."

Natalie raised her eyebrows again.

Ben looked away, then looked back at her and leaned forwards suddenly.

"Look, Natalie..." He forced her to meet his eyes. "You're obviously pissed at me and I don't know why. If I've offended you in some way, I apologise and I'm very happy to try and make amends. But I can't fix something if I don't know what I did wrong. If you're unhappy about something, why not just spit it out? Because I don't deserve this attitude from you. I didn't come out tonight to sit with someone who's gonna snipe at me the whole evening."

Natalie flushed and looked down. A deep sense of shame overcame her. He was right. She had been behaving like a complete cow.

"I... I'm sorry," she mumbled.

Ben smiled slightly. "Hey, no problem. But I feel like somehow we got off on the wrong foot. Let's just start again, okay? And I'd appreciate it if you could drop the constant rock star thing and just start treating me like a regular guy."

Natalie nodded, shamefaced.

Ben nodded at their empty glasses. "Want another drink? And you haven't had any dinner yet, have you? Should I get you something to eat?"

Natalie looked at him gratefully, surprised at his thoughtfulness. "Thanks, yeah—something small will do. Maybe some chips and mayo."

Ben looked puzzled for a moment and Natalie realised why when he returned a few moments later with two beers, a packet of Pringles, and a bottle of mayonnaise that was obviously borrowed from the kitchen.

"I didn't know you Australians like to have mayonnaise with your chips? Seems a bit weird," said Ben, setting the items down on the table.

Natalie laughed in spite of herself. "Not those. We have it with deep-fried potato chips."

"Oh, you mean *fries*," said Ben.

"We call them chips. We call the stuff in packets

'crisps'. And we definitely don't eat them with mayo," Natalie said with a smile.

Ben shook his head, chuckling. "Okay, I'll remember that. I'm still getting my head around some of the other language differences—like yesterday at the resort, I nearly spat my drink out when this woman next to me on the beach asked me if I'd seen her thongs anywhere. Took me a while to realise she meant her flip-flops and not her G-string."

Natalie giggled. "I wish I'd seen your face." She opened the packet and helped herself to some crisps. "So are you finding it really different here compared to back home?"

"I don't know... on the surface, it's not that different. Australia feels a lot like the U.S.—just a cleaner, friendlier, safer version. But there are these little differences that throw you from time to time. Like the way you drive on the other side of the road and the first floor is actually the second floor and your light switches are backwards and you seem to use green for your EXIT signs instead of red... and man, you Aussies really like your slang! Sometimes I wonder if I'm speaking the same language."

Natalie laughed. "It's not that hard. Mostly you just shorten things—like 'uni' for university, 'sunnies' for sunglasses, and 'postie' for postman."

"What about 'cozzie'? What's that got to do with a swimsuit?"

"It's short for 'swimming *costume*'," Natalie

explained. "And you must have heard 'arvo' by now, short for 'afternoon'. We like putting 'o' at the end of words. Like 'servo' for service station and 'bottle-o' for the liquor shop."

"So what do you call jellyfish... 'jell-o'?"

Natalie laughed. "No, we call 'em 'stingers'. And if they're bluebottles, we called them 'blueys'— although a 'bluey' can also be a nickname for a redhead, a blue heeler cattle dog, a traffic ticket, or a type of blanket you take into the outback. You've got to know the context."

"You call red-haired people 'blueys'?" Ben threw his hands up. "I give up." He leaned forwards with a grin. "But I have to say one thing: you Aussies are crap at bacon. You've gotta come to the States and I'll take you to eat some proper thin crispy bacon."

"You're on!" said Natalie, laughing. Then she realised what she had just said and drew back, the laughter dying in her throat. She was enjoying herself *too much* here. She had to remember who Ben was—*what* he was. She was glad that Ben went off to order the chips, giving her a moment alone to compose herself. By the time he was back, she had recovered her composure again and was determined to stay cool and detached: she would be polite and pleasant but that was all.

"So... have you always lived in Summer Beach?" Ben asked as he sat down again.

Natalie nodded.

"Do you think you'd ever want to leave?"

"I don't know... I guess, probably... for work. There are a lot more job opportunities down in Sydney. But I think I'd always come back here eventually."

"Have you got family here?"

"Just my grandmother." Then, feeling a bit rude, she added, "What about you? Do you live near your family back in the States?"

Ben looked down, fiddling with the neck of his beer bottle. "No, I don't have family near me."

Something in the way he said that made Natalie reluctant to ask more. Instead, she said, "What about friends? I reckon you must have a big circle of friends and a busy social life, especially with your career taking off like that."

Ben shrugged. "You make a lot of acquaintances and contacts, sure, but real friends? I probably would count them on the fingers of one hand. And Craig would be one of them. The thing about fame is that suddenly, everybody wants to know you, but you never really know if they want *you* or just a piece of your success." He shook his head. "Sorry, that sounds harsh. Most people I've met in the industry have been pretty decent and several have really supported me. But it's hard to feel close to people sometimes when you're always wondering if they're genuine. Most of my close friends are people I met before I became famous."

He looked up and met Natalie's eyes. "You mentioned earlier about me getting special treatment. Actually, one of the reasons I like Craig is because he doesn't act like I'm some big rock star. He treats me just like a regular guy and he isn't afraid to call me out if I'm out of line."

"Maybe it's because Craig's a celebrity himself so he knows what it's like."

Ben nodded. "Maybe. But it's more than that. You guys seem to have a different attitude to celebrities and I really like that. I mean, everybody loves Craig and he gets a lot of media attention, but people seem to expect him to be really down-to-earth too. Sometimes I feel like he works overtime to show that he's just like everyone else."

Natalie gave a wry laugh. "You're talking about the Tall Poppy Syndrome. Us Aussies don't like it when someone tries to get above themselves. It's a huge part of Australian culture to always stay humble and remember your roots. So if anyone tries to stand up above the rest, we call them 'tall poppies' and cut them down. It's not just celebrities—it goes for everyone. You should always remember that you're 'one of the mates' and no better than anyone else."

"Sounds like a good philosophy to me," said Ben.

The chips arrived, hot and crispy, with a side of garlic mayonnaise and another of tomato sauce, and they put aside Antipodean-American differences in their joint appreciation of junk food. Natalie was surprised when she next looked at her watch and saw that it was nearly eleven o'clock.

Where had the evening gone? She didn't want to admit it, but she hadn't enjoyed herself this much in a long time.

They were silent on the car ride back to the resort, although this time it was a silence of comfortable companionship. As they pulled up in front of the resort's main entrance, Ben turned to her and said, "Thanks very much for tonight. I know you were just doing it as a favour for Craig, but I had a great time."

"Me too." Natalie smiled shyly. "Look... I'm actually not doing anything tomorrow afternoon. Do you... Do you want to do a bit more sightseeing? I'd be happy to show you around the area."

Ben paused in the act of getting out of the car and turned to look at her. "It's okay. You don't have to feel like you need to do anything more with me—"

"No, I want to do it. I'd like to show you around," Natalie insisted.

"In that case... Thanks, I'd love that." His teeth flashed in the darkness of the car interior. "But can I make a special request?"

"Yes?"

"Can we not go to any more bars?"

Natalie looked at him in surprise. "What would you like to do then?"

"How about a hike? You must have some really beautiful tracks around here. I'd love to see some of the coast."

"Oh." Natalie stared at him in surprise. "Er...

Sure… I just didn't think you would…"

"What?" Ben raised an amused eyebrow.

"I just didn't think you'd be into things like hiking and outdoor stuff," said Natalie lamely.

Ben laugh and shook his head. "I don't know where you got your ideas about rock stars from—maybe you've watched too many Hollywood movies—but a lot of us aren't drugged-out alcoholics who are constantly in rehab and need sex therapy. We're just normal people who like to make music. At least, I am."

Natalie gave a sheepish laugh. "Okay. If you're really up to it, there's a great walking track along the coast in the Wyrrabalong National Park. It includes a fantastic lookout where you can often see whales on their northern migration."

"Sounds awesome," said Ben. "When do you want me to be ready?"

"How about here, tomorrow, at two o'clock?"

"Can't wait," he said enthusiastically. "Thanks again for tonight." He got out of the car and slammed the door.

Natalie watched him disappear into the resort, then started for home, her mind filled with excitement at the thought of tomorrow.

CHAPTER TEN

Sara smiled as she watched her parents talking and laughing with her aunt and uncle and her two brothers as they relaxed on the terrace of Craig's house. It was so surreal seeing her family here in Australia, but it was great to have them all together again. Ever since her two brothers had moved to the East Coast, family get-togethers were pretty rare.

As if reading her thoughts, her mother looked across at her and said, "Honey, isn't it ironic that we've had to come halfway across the world to finally get everyone together at last?"

"And we nearly got sent back because of your mother's smuggling habits," grumbled Sara's father.

"Oh, please—they wouldn't have deported us for that." Mrs Monroe waved a hand dismissively. "Sara told me she really missed the brownies from back home so I thought I'd make her some and bring them."

"That was really sweet of you, Mom, but I told you not to bring in any fresh food," said Sara reproachfully. "Remember I told you how strict they are about quarantine here in Australia? You're lucky you didn't get fined thousands of dollars."

"Oh, I almost didn't mind getting caught," laughed Mrs Monroe. "Because I got to meet this gorgeous little detector dog. She was a Beagle and she looked a bit like Coco."

At the sound of her name, Coco looked up and wagged her tail. She had been nose down under the coffee table, busily sniffing for crumbs.

"I can't believe they let dogs roam around like that in the airport," said Sara's Aunt Sophie with a disgusted expression. "Imagine all the germs they're carrying around! And what if they poop and pee on the floor?"

"I'm sure they're well trained," said Sara, trying not to let her irritation show. Her aunt's disapproval of animals was something she should have been used to by now—she had come across it often enough throughout her childhood, every time she had gone over to play with Ellie. But she still found the attitude frustrating. It was no wonder, really, that Ellie had grown up with such an aversion to dogs. It had taken one mischievous Labrador—and a sexy veterinarian, Sara thought with a smile—to help her cousin change her mind.

She cringed inwardly at the thought of her aunt finding out that Coco would be coming to the wedding. It had been hard enough having Aunt Sophie accept that Coco was an inside dog and was given free run of the house. She saw her aunt watching the Beagle askance now as the dog peeked over the top of the coffee table, looking hopefully for any food close enough to grab. Coco's soft hound lips draped over the edge of the table, leaving a thin trail of drool on the surface.

"Hey, Coco... come away, girl," Sara said hastily, leaning over to wipe the corner of the table with a napkin.

"Well, I'm happy to have made the fourteen-hour trip if only to taste this beer," said Jake Monroe, Sara's oldest brother, with a grin. He held the bottle up and examined the label. "This is really good. Where's it from?"

"It's from a microbrewery, I think. You know how the Aussies are into their craft beers. Craig really likes this brand. It's named after a convict called James Squire who was supposed to have opened Australia's first brewery."

"Quirky history as well as great flavour," said Sara's other brother, Ryan, with a smirk. He finished his bottle and got up. "Where's Craig? He said he was going to get a few more bottles, but he hasn't come back. Maybe I should go and—"

"I'll go," said Sara, standing up. "I need to grab a sweater anyway—it's getting a bit chilly out here."

The wraparound terrace of Craig's house gave a great view of the sea and the beach below, but it could also be really windy. Sara rubbed her bare arms and shivered in the strong breeze blowing in off the ocean. She went back into the house and made her way down the hallway to the kitchen. As she stepped in, she was surprised to see Craig and Ellie huddled by the counter, their heads together over something. Their backs were to her and she couldn't see what they were looking at, but she could hear the tone of concern in their voices.

"Hey…"

They both jumped and turned around. Ellie snatched something behind her back.

"What's going on?" asked Sara.

"Nothing" said Ellie quickly with a breezy smile on her face.

"You're a lousy liar, Ellie," said Sara, walking up to her cousin and trying to peer behind her back. "What have you got there?"

"It's nothing!" said Ellie, backing away from her. "Just some stupid… work stuff…"

"Then why were you and Craig looking at it?" Sara turned to look at her fiancé, who gave an awkward shrug. "Are you guys hiding something from me?" she demanded.

Ellie glanced at Craig, biting her lip. Then she gave a big sigh and pulled her arms from behind her back. "All right. But I don't want you to freak out. You've got to remember, this is just the paparazzi doing what they're good at..."

Sara stepped forwards to see what her cousin had laid on the counter. Her eyes widened with horror as she took in the magazine cover in front of her. It was a picture of herself down at the beach. Her back was to the camera and she was bending over to pick up a tennis ball. In the background, you could see Coco standing, one paw raised, eyes bright and waiting for the ball. But what Sara zoomed in on was the close-up of her backside in the foreground, with her shorts riding up her thighs and her cellulite in full view. Next to it was a headline which said:

"Aussie Beach Vet's overweight bride desperate to get in shape before the wedding!"

Sara paled. "Oh my God..."

She flipped the magazine open and found the story. It was a double-page spread, with several photos of her on the beach, each more unflattering than the last. They were all blurry and looked like stills taken from a video. Underneath the collage of photos was a short paragraph which read:

TV heartthrob Dr Craig Murray may be ready for his big day next week, but it looks like his American bride is making a last-minute desperate attempt to shed the extra pounds. Seen pounding the beach with her dog, Sara Monroe was obviously worried about her figure and whether she will fit into her dress on the day. Sources suggest that she has been sticking to a strict diet of vegetable juices and organic rice crackers to trim her curvy figure, while using self-hypnosis and tantric meditation to curb the hunger pangs. Will she lose the weight in time for the big day? Catch all the behind-the-scenes action in the special feature Aussie Beach Vet: Wedding Bells, coming soon to your TV screens!

Ellie snatched the magazine away from her. "Don't read that. You know it's just a bunch of nonsense they make up. I mean, that stuff about vegetable juices and tantric meditation is just laughable—"

"These were taken during my walk with Coco the day before yesterday," said Sara through clenched teeth. "That film crew said they were just getting footage for the wedding feature. They never said they were going to sell the photos to magazines!"

"I know, I know... I've spoken to Jenn about it already," said Craig, holding his hands up in a placating gesture. "She's really apologetic. She didn't write that copy; she just gave some stills to the magazine and asked that they mention the show. She thought a story might be a great way to generate some buzz—a sort of teaser—before the show aired. But she never thought they'd take this angle about your weight and figure. She didn't realise you'd be so sensitive—"

"What do you mean 'so sensitive'?" shrieked Sara. "Which woman wouldn't be sensitive about seeing herself plastered like that all over a magazine?"

"Sara—" said Ellie soothingly.

"Don't you *dare* tell me to embrace my curves!" snapped Sara. "You're not the one being humiliated with your butt the size of Brazil and all your cellulite on show for the world to ogle at."

Craig picked up the magazine and frowned. "What cellulite? I don't think you look that bad, sweetheart—"

"AARRRGHH!" Sara stared at him disbelievingly. Could men really be that obtuse?

"Sorry... I'm sorry, Sara, and Jenn is too. She swears it won't happen again. She really didn't realise the magazine would spin the story like that. She's not going to be providing them with any more images unless you approve them," said Craig, reaching out to put an arm around her shoulders.

Sara shrugged him off and stalked to the door. She turned back and glared at him.

"You're damned right it won't happen again. Because if it does, it's not just the show that would be cancelled... it's the whole wedding!"

CHAPTER ELEVEN

"How did the evening go with Ben last night?" Rita Walker asked as she and Natalie were finishing lunch the next day.

Natalie kept her gaze studiously on her plate. "It was fine. We went to a couple of bars and pubs in Newcastle. And I'm meeting him again this afternoon," she added casually.

"Oh?" Rita said, the corners of her mouth curling up in a smile.

"It's just for a small hike," Natalie said quickly. "He mentioned yesterday he'd really like to see some of the coastline so I thought we'd take a walk up to Crackneck Lookout. I mean, he's only visiting Oz for a short while and it would be a shame if he didn't see some of the bush. I'm really just helping Craig and Sara with one of their wedding guests..." She glanced at her grandmother. "You don't mind, do you Gran? I didn't think we were doing anything special this afternoon."

"Oh, no, of course I don't mind," said Rita, smiling. "I was actually planning to go out this arvo to the bowls club anyway—Graham is coming to pick me up."

"Bowls? But what about your hips—"

"Oh, I won't play," said Rita. "But it'll be nice to go and have a chinwag with some of the other regulars. And Graham will bring me back so there's no need for you to worry. You don't have to rush back for me. In fact, why don't you take Ben to the Laughing Kookaburra afterwards? Make sure he tries some proper Aussie fish and chips."

"Sounds like a good idea," said Natalie as she got up from the table. She dropped a kiss on her grandmother's cheek and ran off to get changed.

It took a lot longer than usual to choose her outfit, but Natalie told herself it was important to make a good impression. *For professional reasons, of course. Not because I'm trying to impress Ben or anything,* she thought hastily. After much deliberation, she donned a pair of jeans with a turtleneck sweater and a fleece vest, finishing off with woolly socks and chunky hiking boots. She pulled her long brown hair into a soft plait at the side of her neck and added a touch of makeup: mascara, tinted sunscreen, and lip gloss.

She eyed herself critically in the mirror. Her

cheeks were flushed and her eyes sparkled with anticipation. She saw her grandmother do a double take when she went downstairs and braced herself for a comment, but Rita simply smiled and said:

"Don't forget the binoculars."

"Thanks, Gran."

Natalie snagged the binoculars from the hook beside the front door and waved goodbye. She felt wonderfully carefree as she drove to the resort. It was absurd, but she couldn't remember the last time she had looked forward to an outing so much. It was nothing to do with Ben's company, of course—it was just that she had been working so hard lately and it was nice to have an afternoon off.

Still, she couldn't ignore the way her heart skipped a beat when she pulled up in front of the resort and Ben got into the car. He looked cool and rugged and incredibly handsome in a wool sweater and dark jeans, with sturdy hiking boots. A whiff of his tangy citrus cologne wafted towards her and Natalie was suddenly aware again of how close they were inside the car.

"It's a great day, isn't it? The weather is meant to be really good and we'll get great views from the lookouts; this is one of the most beautiful walks on the Central Coast and it's especially nice in winter, not that it's not great in summer too, of course..." Natalie realised that she was babbling. She stopped and took a deep breath as she saw Ben watching her in amusement.

She took another breath and said, more calmly, "Are you sure you're up to this? I mean, with the injury on your leg. The track's about a six kilometre round trip."

"That's nothing," said Ben. "I go for a lot of long hikes back home in the States. There are some beautiful tracks up in the Catskills and I go whenever I can. Yeah," he said with a laugh at her look. "Like I told you, I don't spend all my time at bars and clubs wrecking my liver."

They arrived at Wyrrabalong National Park in good time and parked by Forresters Beach, then set off on the Coast Track. Natalie was pleasantly surprised to discover that Ben was a good walker—in fact, he easily outstripped her and she had to hurry to keep up with his long strides. Somehow, the image of an athletic, down-to-earth nature lover didn't quite fit with her idea of a rock star either, but she was beginning to realise that she would have to seriously revise her image of Ben Falco.

The first section of the track followed the narrow beach between the cliffs and the water—but this was not a soft white sand beach like the one by the resort. This was a rocky shoreline full of craggy boulders and strange rock formations—stark and beautiful in a different way. It was tough going, with a lot of rock-hopping and climbing over the rocky ledges. Waves crashed on their right, spraying them with salt water, and there was a sense of exhilaration at how exposed they were to the ocean—in fact, they were lucky that it was low tide otherwise this section of beach would have been impassable.

They didn't talk much, each concentrating on scrambling across the slippery rocks, but Natalie felt a sense of companionship that she had never felt before. Somehow, Ben always seemed to know when she needed a helping hand or wanted to pause to admire a particular view.

"Strange to see these here," commented Ben, pointing to several old engine blocks and other car parts lying among the rocks.

"They've always been here, as long as I can remember," said Natalie. "You'd think they look awful—like rubbish on the beach—but actually, they're so old and rusty, they seem to be almost part of the landscape." She paused and shaded her eyes against the sun with one hand, peering ahead. "We're almost at Crackneck Beach now."

They soon arrived at a small beach which was covered with rocks the size of a fist, each one worn smooth by the sea. It looked almost like a giant hand had scattered giant M&M's across the shoreline. Ben picked one up and ran his fingers over it admiringly.

"Almost wish I could take one back as a souvenir."

"Don't you have rocks in the U.S.?" Natalie teased.

"Yeah, but somehow they don't feel as exotic."

Ben grinned.

They continued along the beach, which gradually smoothed out to a more conventional sandy shoreline as they reached the south end of Bateau Bay Beach. A series of steps led up to the top of the cliffs, where the track continued on the circular route back to Forresters Beach, following the cliffs above the shore. It was easier going now, with a gentle climb that meandered through the lush coastal rainforest. Every so often, the bush on their left would part to reveal a glimpse of the sparkling sea stretching to the horizon, and all around them rose the strange, alien-like silhouettes of the cabbage tree palms, sharp against the vivid blue sky.

Natalie pulled the binoculars from around her neck as they reached Crackneck Lookout and handed them to Ben.

"Go on—take a squizz. See if you can spot any whales."

Ben looped the binoculars over his own neck, then raised them and scanned the sea. The lookout had a 180-degree view of the ocean and was one of the best spots on the Central Coast for whale-watching from land.

Natalie fidgeted next to him. "See anything?"

"No... Nothing..." Ben turned slowly, moving the binoculars across the seascape.

"Keep looking... I'm sure they're there."

"So which kinds can you see?"

"There are usually a lot of humpbacks passing this time of year, although people say sometimes you can see a southern right whale. But they're really rare. I've never seen one." Natalie walked to the edge of the lookout and shaded her eyes, looking out to the ocean. "They're coming up from Antarctica where they feed for most of the year— they migrate to Australia, where the water's warmer, to breed. If you go up to Queensland, you'll see a lot of whales off the shore there."

Ben smirked at her. "Did you do whales as a school project or something?"

Natalie laughed. "No, I just always found them fascinating. I did have this teacher at school who was really into whales—she was a member of the Whale and Dolphin Conservation Society and always writing letters to governments protesting about whaling and stuff. I guess some of it rubbed off on me." She came back to his side. "You know the humpback whale is a spiritual totem animal for a lot of the indigenous Aboriginal tribes? They're sacred to the Darkinjung People here in the Central Coast, for instance, and there's a tribe down in South Australia called the Mirning who've been carrying out 'whale dreaming' ceremonies for centuries. They hold it at Whale Rock on the Great Australian Bight, which is shaped like a whale's tail. They believe that it's a gateway to the stars and their dreamtime connects their past, present, and future together in one dream. And when they die, it is with the whale that they return to the stars."

"That's... quite beautiful," said Ben.

Natalie nodded. "And they have an amazing member who is a 'Whale Whisperer'—he has a special gift: he can call to the whales and they'll respond and come to the shore. I didn't believe it, but there was a documentary made about him and I saw him actually do it. It was pretty incredible."

Ben lowered his binoculars and stared at her. "D'you know... I think I've heard about him! His name is Bunna Lawrie, isn't it? He was in an indigenous rock band from the 80's called the Coloured Stones. I found them when I was going through a second-hand music store—I really like their stuff."

"Probably. I don't follow the music scene much."

Ben looked at her in surprise. "Really? The way you were singing in the car the other day, I would have thought you'd be really into music."

Natalie shrugged, then pointed at the binoculars and said, with an attempt at lightness, "We're here to see whales, not talk about music."

Ben regarded her thoughtfully for a moment, then put the binoculars to his eyes and turned back to the sea. "Nothing... nothing yet... Maybe it's the wrong time of day and they—Wait...!"

Natalie looked eagerly at him.

"Yeah, I think... yes, there's a tail!" Ben said excitedly. "Quick—take a look!"

He lowered the binoculars and offered them to

her, but because they were still looped around his neck, Natalie had to lean close to him to line her eyes up to the eyecups. Ben shifted position and put an arm around her shoulders to give her better access. Natalie felt her pulse jump and found it hard to concentrate on what was in the lens.

"Do you see it?" Ben's breath was warm against her ear.

"Um..." Natalie tried to gather her scattered thoughts. The tantalising scent of his aftershave wafted over her again and she felt the heat of his body through the layers of clothing between them. "I'm not sure..."

Then something dark flickered in the centre of the lens and Natalie's attention snapped back to the image in the binoculars. "Oh! Yes! I see it!" she cried. "A tail! Yes, it's a humpback! It just breached and did the most fantastic jump!"

She turned excitedly towards Ben and found herself suddenly very close, their lips inches apart. She froze. The air between them seemed to hum with an electric charge. Ben's eyes darkened and his gaze dropped to her lips.

Natalie trembled. Was he going to kiss her? Did she want him to?

Then the moment passed. Ben dropped his arm and stepped slowly away from her, easing the binoculars out of her hands. Natalie felt hot colour come to her cheeks. She turned away and fiddled with the zipper of her fleece vest.

"Um... now that you've seen a whale, I think we should push on. Still got half the walk to do."

Ben nodded and fell into step behind her as she led the way. They walked the rest of the route in silence, pausing only once more to take in the view at Wyrrabalong Lookout.

"I think this is one of the most beautiful walks I've ever been on," Ben said, his gaze on the sea.

"It's a shame you won't be here a few months from now—this track is gorgeous in the spring. There are wildflowers blooming everywhere."

"I could always come back."

Natalie glanced quickly at him, her heart thudding in her chest. "Oh... I thought... well, without Craig's wedding, you wouldn't really have a reason to come all the way to Australia, would you?"

Ben gave her a sideways look, a smile tugging at the corners of his mouth. "Oh, I think I might have a reason to come back."

He turned to face her and reached out slowly to brush back a strand of hair which had come loose from her plait. Natalie felt the touch of his fingers on her brow, soft and lingering, almost like a caress. She stared up into his eyes, her breath coming faster. She tried to remember all the reasons why Ben Falco was bad for her, why she had to stay away from him, but they were like dim voices, fading away in the distance. Much louder was the thumping of her heart and the rushing of blood in her ears as he lowered his head slowly towards her. Natalie shut her eyes, holding her breath in anticipation.

Then a rustle in the bushes nearby made them both jump apart.

"G'day!" A smiling middle-aged man and his wife stepped from the track onto the lookout area and nodded to them in a friendly way.

"Um... Hi..." Natalie stammered, giving them a distracted smile.

She backed away from Ben, horrified now at what had nearly happened. What had she been thinking? How could she have let him almost kiss her?

"We... we should keep going... otherwise it'll be dark by the time we make it back to the car," she said, hurrying to join the track again and not looking to see if he was following her.

CHAPTER TWELVE

Ben stared at Natalie's dark head as she walked ahead of him. He could still feel the silk of her hair between his fingers and see, in his mind's eye, the way her soft pink lips had parted and her eyelids fluttered shut when he had leaned towards her. He cursed the bad timing of those other hikers again.

Maybe it was for the best, though, he thought. He wasn't sure if kissing Natalie was the right thing to do. It would complicate things even further—and things were confusing enough. He was sure he hadn't mistaken the sizzling attraction between them and he was sure Natalie felt it too. She didn't seem like the type to play 'hard to get' and yet he had never received such mixed signals from another girl before: one minute she seemed warm and willing, her face alight with that heart-melting smile, and the next minute she was pulling away, her eyes haunted and scared. *What was she scared of?*

Ben knew that he shouldn't pursue this. He was only going to be in Australia for a few more days—it was crazy to even think of a possible future together. And yet that was exactly what he was thinking. In fact, it was the only thing he had been thinking about ever since that first morning when he had met Natalie on the beach.

Ben glanced at her again, admiring the way the late afternoon sun caught the red highlights in her hair and the way the faded fabric of her jeans moulded to the curve of her hips and the graceful line of her legs. Even though she was dressed down today, with a face that seemed bare of make-up, she was gorgeous, with a fresh, girl-next-door sort of beauty that was enhanced by her simple appearance.

But it wasn't just her looks. Ben was used to beautiful girls. Even before his career had taken off, he had had more than his fair share of attractive models throwing themselves at him. But none of them had touched him the way Natalie had, with her soft Australian drawl and her quiet beauty. And there was a vulnerability in her eyes that made him want to take her into his arms and keep her safe from the world.

Ben shook his head and laughed to himself. Who was he kidding? The truth was, he had fallen for

Natalie. Hard. And it didn't matter that they lived thousands of miles apart or came from totally different cultures—he wanted to find some way for them to be together.

If only he could find some way to get her to open up to him, to tell him what she was scared of! Suddenly, he was determined to try. They might only have a few days left, but he would do his damnedest to win Natalie over in the time he had. He wouldn't give up and go back to the States without at least trying and giving it his all.

Ben had been expecting Natalie to take him back to the resort straightaway, so he was pleasantly surprised when she asked hesitantly if he would like to stop for some fish and chips.

"Yeah, I'd love that," said Ben. "I've had fish and chips a few times in the States, but I don't know how authentic it was."

"Well, my grandmother would never forgive me if I didn't take you to try the real thing," said Natalie with a smile. "I was going to take you to the Laughing Kookaburra—that's a café back in Summer Beach which does some of the best seafood in the Central Coast. But it's a long drive back. Might be better to find somewhere close to here."

They stopped off in Woy Woy at the Fisherman's Wharf and got big helpings of crispy fried fish with thick fries—*or chips, as Natalie calls them*, Ben reminded himself with a smile—and carried their purchases to the park in front of the shop. There, they found a bench with a view overlooking the water and sat down to eat whilst watching the boats pass by.

Ben unwrapped his steaming parcel and bit into his fish—it was absolutely delicious: soft and flaky, covered in a thick crispy batter and done to perfection. He took another big bite, suddenly ravenous. He didn't think he had ever eaten fish cooked so simply yet which tasted so good.

"You've got to put some tomato sauce on it," said Natalie, offering him a sachet with a teasing smile. "Nothing's eaten properly in Australia unless it's got tomato sauce on it."

Ben swallowed and grinned. "No thanks—this is amazing the way it is. What's this fish?"

"It's barramundi," said Natalie. "Probably the most popular fish in Australia."

Ben picked up a chip and popped it in his mouth. They were golden and crispy on the outside, fluffy on the inside, and liberally sprinkled with salt.

"These are amazing," he said as he licked his fingers.

Natalie chuckled. "Yeah, they beat the ones from Maccas, don't they?"

"Maccas?" Ben looked at her quizzically.

"McDonald's," Natalie explained.

Ben made a face of mock exasperation. "Now,

you can't tell me that Maccas sounds anything like McDonald's!"

Natalie giggled. "Okay, I admit that one's a bit weird. But every Aussie knows it so I guess we never think about it."

A seagull called raucously next to them and they noticed suddenly that a small group of the cheeky birds had congregated around them. A few rose in the air and hovered above them, eyeing the packets on their laps with interest.

"Better watch out," Natalie said. "They can be right little buggers."

"What do you mea—Hey!" Ben yelled as a seagull suddenly swooped down and snatched a chip right out of his fingers.

Natalie burst out laughing "I told you!"

"Ah well... I've pretty much finished anyway," said Ben, putting the last chip into his mouth and rolling the remnants of paper wrapping up.

He stood up and held his hand out to Natalie, who had copied his example with her food. He pulled her to her feet and they stood for a moment, staring at each other. He didn't let her hand go. Seagulls called above them and, in the distance, they could hear the faint rumble of a boat engine *put-putting* softly across the water. The orange rays of the setting run touched the delicate features of Natalie's face, highlighting her cheekbones and the sweet curve of her chin. She looked up at him, her eyes wide, then her lips parted and she swayed slightly towards him.

The next moment a white flash went off, blinding them. Natalie gasped, and staggered backwards slightly, her hands up to her eyes. Ben put an arm protectively around her as he squinted around them. A couple more flashes went off in quick succession, then as the blindness faded, Ben made out the shape of a man standing a few feet away from them, holding a large camera with a telephoto lens. He swore under his breath.

"Wh...what's going on? Is someone taking our picture?" asked Natalie, blinking in confusion.

"Come on, let's get back to the car," said Ben briskly, putting a gentle hand under her elbow.

He hustled Natalie back to their vehicle and they got in, with the sound of camera shutters clicking rapidly behind them. As Natalie reversed out of their space, Ben saw the man jump into a car parked nearby.

He swore again. "He's going to try to follow us."

"Let him," said Natalie grimly, flooring the accelerator.

She zoomed down the main road through the town and turned suddenly down a side street, then made a few more turns until Ben was completely confused which direction they were heading in. It seemed like the man following them was too—at least, he was no longer visible behind them.

"Looks like you've lost him," said Ben, throwing a glance over his shoulder at the rear window of the car. "Sorry about that. I guess the paparazzi must have found out where I am after all. I wonder how long it'll take them to work out that I'm staying at Summer Beach Resort."

"Well, at least we can try to make it harder for them. I won't go on the freeway—I can take an alternative route back," said Natalie. "It cuts through the bush so it'll take a bit longer, but we'll be pretty sure we won't meet anyone."

Ben nodded. "Sounds like a good idea."

Night had fallen now, and the country road wasn't as well lit as the motorway. The tarmac stretched ahead of them into the darkness beyond the headlights and the open bush around them passed as a grey blur outside the car windows, interrupted only by the occasional black forms of tall gum trees.

A yellow road sign flashed past with a black animal silhouette in the middle and Ben did a double take. "Did that sign just show a kangaroo?"

Natalie flicked her eyes to the rear-view mirror. "Yes, why?"

"You see them on postcards and things, but I thought they were just a joke or put up for tourists!"

"No, they're real road signs. There are wild kangaroos in the countryside around here and you have to be careful when you're driving, especially at night."

"You're not serious." Ben grinned. "What—do

they just hop out into the middle of the road?"

"I *am* serious," said Natalie. "A big male roo can get up to two metres tall and weigh two hundred pounds. It's not funny if you hit one. They can wreck your car and there have been some fatal collisions. A lot of rural people have bulbars on their cars if they do a lot of driving around the countryside at night. Or, as we call it, roo bars." She glanced at Ben. "Don't you have big animals that wander onto roads in the States?"

"Well, now that you mention it, yeah—I guess you get moose and elk if you're up in the northern... To be honest, though, I think you're more likely to hit another car than anything else."

"Yeah, that goes for here too," Natalie said wryly. "Especially as you can get your licence at sixteen. I mean, it might just be a provisional licence, so you can only drive if someone with a full licence sits in the car with you. But you know, that 'someone' could be just a few years older than you and not necessarily more responsible..."

Ben shook his head. "Yeah, same in the States. Our drinking age is higher, though."

"I think the U.S. has one of the highest drinking ages, doesn't it?"

"Not that anyone really waits till twenty-one," said Ben dryly. "I can remember—LOOK OUT!"

He lunged across and grabbed the steering wheel, yanking it to one side as the car veered away from a huge grey shape that had loomed out of the darkness. They heard a faint thud against the front fender, just as Natalie braked hard and they screeched to a halt.

They both sat for a moment, breathing heavily, their pulses racing. Through the front windshield, Ben could see several dark shapes moving across the road in front of them. He blinked. They were *bouncing*.

Natalie gave a shaky laugh. "Okay, I wasn't looking for such a scary way to prove my point, but yeah, that sign we saw a while back? Not just for tourists. Here are the roos."

Ben stared at the big marsupials. He had seen pictures of kangaroos, of course, and everyone had teased him about seeing them when he'd mentioned that he was coming to Australia. In fact, he had been fully expecting to see one—but in a zoo or some kind of wildlife park. Not just hopping across the road in front of him. It all felt slightly surreal.

One large kangaroo paused in the middle of the road and turned to look directly at the car, blinking myopically in the glare of the headlights. She had huge, long ears, almost like a donkey, and large docile eyes with thick lashes. She stood upright, leaning back on her tail, and sniffed the air curiously, her small clawed hands tucked close against her chest.

"It's a doe..." Natalie whispered. "Look, she's got a joey."

As Ben watched, a little furry head popped

suddenly out of the pouch and looked around curiously. The baby was a perfect miniature replica of its mother and it stretched out one spindly leg from the pouch opening. The doe bent over and nuzzled the baby's head, then turned and hopped on.

Ben let out the breath he had been holding. "Okay, *that* was the most awesome moment."

Natalie smiled as she watched the rest of the mob move off the road and into the adjoining field. "I'm glad you got to see that. Would have been real shame if you'd come to Australia and not seen a kangaroo."

"Yeah, but this beats seeing them in a zoo." Ben shook his head with a laugh. "There's something almost... magical about seeing an animal in the wild. Seriously, I feel so high right now... I don't think I'll ever forget this night."

Natalie eased the car forwards again. She spoke so softly, he almost thought he imagined it but he caught the words as she turned back to the steering wheel: "Neither will I."

CHAPTER THIRTEEN

Natalie shut the front door silently behind her and tiptoed across the darkened living room. She headed up the stairs and was about to cross the hallway to her bedroom when she noticed that the light was on in her grandmother's room. Just in case Rita had been waiting up for her, she turned and went towards the lit doorway.

"So you're back." Rita smiled as she took off her spectacles. She was sitting in bed, propped up against the pillows, a book on her lap. "Good time?"

Natalie drifted over and sat down at the foot of her bed. "Yes... I had a great time."

"Where did you go?"

"We did the Coast Track in Wyrrabalong and then we had fish and chips down in Woy Woy, and then we had this amazing kangaroo encounter on the road on the way back." She sighed. "I almost didn't want it to end..."

Her grandmother looked at her shrewdly. "How long is Ben staying in Australia?"

"He's only come for the wedding." Natalie looked down at her hands. "But he... he said today that he might come back."

Rita raised her eyebrows. "And you'd like that?"

Natalie sighed. "I don't know... I don't know, Gran, I don't know! I know it's all wrong and I shouldn't even be spending time with him! But when I'm with him, I feel so..." She trailed off, unable to put it into words.

Her grandmother frowned. "Why shouldn't you be spending time with him, possum?"

"Because he's a rock star! He's really big in the States and probably going to get more famous and successful and—"

"Natalie..." Rita said gently. "You're not your mother—"

"How do you know?" Natalie asked wildly. "How do you know I wouldn't be exactly like her?"

Before her grandmother could answer, she sprang up from the bed and ran from the room.

"Natalie?" Sara's voice sounded impatient.

Natalie jumped and came back to the present. She had been daydreaming about her time with Ben yesterday—something she had been doing repeatedly. In fact, she had been struggling to keep her mind on work the whole day. Her thoughts kept drifting to Ben at every opportunity. *What was he doing now? Had he thought about her as much as she had thought about him? Had yesterday been as special to him?*

She adjusted the phone next to her ear. "Sorry, Sara—I missed the last part. Would you mind repeating that again?"

"My idea for a Tim Tam cake! I know we'd already agreed on the wedding cake, but I had this idea last night and I thought Tim Tams were one of the things that brought Craig and I together. I want our cake to have special meaning—like Ru and the carved seahorses. Do you think Jean-Pierre will be really pissed off?"

Natalie thought of the temperamental French chef who was head of the resort kitchens. She could just imagine what a colourful response she was going to get when she told him about the last-minute change. But she put on her most reassuring tone.

"I'm sure he'd love the challenge," she said diplomatically. "Don't worry, I'll speak to him now."

"Oh, would you? That would be awesome. I'd pop over and come with you, but I've got a final dress fitting and also an appointment with the hairstylist this afternoon. She's been off sick so I've had to postpone the consult to today."

"It's no problem at all," said Natalie. "I'll ring you

later and give you an update."

She put the phone down, took a deep breath, then picked it up again and dialled the internal number for the resort kitchens. She told Jean-Pierre about Sara's request, bracing herself for his outburst, but to her surprise, the French chef seemed to relish the idea.

"Ah, it will be a challenge, *bien sûr...*" he said thoughtfully. "Hmm... *oui... oui...* one will have to build the biscuits into the base and infuse the caramel flavour into cream filling... and of course, melt some of the chocolate fudge coating for the top of the cake... hmm... it is a complex matter... but I shall enjoy it! *Bon.* I will take it on! You can tell Mademoiselle Monroe that I will make her Teem Tam wedding cake—the first of its kind!"

"Thank you so much, Jean-Pierre—I know she will really appreciate it. It will have such special meaning for the wedding."

"*D'accord*, and the rest of the menu? She is happy with that? She does not want to change that, *non*?"

"Oh no, the rest of the menu is fine," said Natalie.

"Ah... because I have created some new canapés. *Oui*, these are exquisite! And they would be wonderful for the wedding! *Alors*, why don't you come now and try them? Come to the bistro—I will tell them to set aside a table for you. Then you can tell Mademoiselle Monroe and she can decide if she wants to change some of her choices for the new ones."

"Well..." Natalie glanced down at her desktop diary, then at the clock on the wall. It was almost lunchtime and she did have to eat. Besides, the thought of trying out some gourmet canapés for lunch was a lot more inviting than her usual hastily gulped sandwich.

"Thanks, Jean-Pierre—I'd love that. I'll see you in a minute."

She hung up and got up from her desk, grabbing her handbag. Then she hesitated and sat back down. She stared at her phone, then picked it up on an impulse. She gave a name to reception and a few minute later she heard Ben's deep voice on the line.

"Oh... I... um... I wasn't sure if you'd be in your room..." she stammered, suddenly flustered now that she was speaking to him.

"I was just on my way down to grab some lunch. I'm glad you called—I've been thinking of you."

Natalie blushed and was glad that he couldn't see her. She didn't quite know how to answer.

"I was thinking of calling you, actually," Ben continued. "But I wasn't sure about disturbing you at work—"

"Oh, well, I'm sort of calling about that," said Natalie quickly, glad of the lead-in he gave her. "I'm just popping down to the bistro to taste some new canapés for the wedding menu and... and I was wondering if you'd like to come with me?"

"Try and stop me!" said Ben with a laugh.

Natalie hung up and stared at the phone again. What was she doing? Then she recalled her grandmother's words from the night before: *"You're not your mother."*

I'm not—I'm not her, she thought fiercely. *This doesn't have to be history repeating itself.*

With that thought churning in her mind, she got up and left the room.

Natalie felt her heart give a leap as she met Ben in the lobby. He was looking relaxed and coolly-attractive in a pair of chinos and a crisp cotton shirt. He smiled at her and she felt a sudden shyness overtake her again. But as they walked together to the beachfront bistro, she gradually felt the familiar closeness from yesterday surround them again.

Natalie was a bit unsure how Jean-Pierre would react when he learned that she had invited an extra mouth to feed, but when he saw Ben, he beamed benevolently. Natalie smiled wryly to herself. She knew that Jean-Pierre had taken a paternal interest in her from their first meeting and the Frenchman had frequently bemoaned her lack of love life. Now she could see a speculative gleam in his eye as he led them into the restaurant and wondered if he was embracing the role of matchmaker.

Her suspicions were confirmed in a moment

when the French chef told the waiter to swap their table to one overlooking the pool outside, and announced they were to have the full *dégustation* menu.

"But I thought you just wanted us to taste a couple your new canapés!" protested Natalie.

"What is the rush? Stay! Eat! Enjoy yourself!" Jean-Pierre said with a majestic wave of his hand. Then with a wink at Ben, he turned and left them alone.

The next hour was occupied with sampling and eating a variety of delicious concoctions which seemed to come in a never-ending stream from the kitchen. Little pizettes with cherry tomatoes, basil and mozzarella, Sydney rock oysters with chardonnay vinegar, roasted fig tarts with goat cheese, pork and fennel sausage rolls with spicy tomato relish, caramelised duck and spring onions in rice paper rolls with plum dipping sauce... At last, just as they thought they would burst, the flow of food came to a stop and they were presented with the options for dessert.

"I can't eat another thing," declared Natalie, leaning back in her chair.

"Uh-huh... me too," Ben agreed. "How about a walk on the beach then, to help the food go down?"

Natalie agreed and they made their way past the pool, down to the beach. They walked for a bit in silence, their feet sinking into the soft sand, the sea breeze stirring their hair.

"Your hair looks reddish in the sun," Ben observed, his eyes on her head. "Anyone have red hair in your family?"

Natalie hesitated, then said, "My mother was a redhead."

"You mean a bluey?" said Ben with a smile.

Natalie gave him a tight smile, then quickly changed the subject. "So what made you decide to become a musician?"

Ben shrugged. "I can't really tell you. I guess it's a little bit like being a writer or an actor—it's a calling, really, more than a conscious career decision. Hell, if I wanted a sensible career, rock music is definitely not what I would have chosen! When I think of the tables I've waited on, the odd jobs I did, the gigs I played, and the long days and nights working on demos to send out to record companies before I got my big break..." He shook his head and gave a rueful laugh. "It's not for the fainthearted."

They walked on in silence for a bit, then Ben said, "What about you? What made you decide to become an event coordinator?"

"It's not really the event coordinator role that I'm interested in," said Natalie. "What I really want to be is a wedding planner. But most people do a bit of event planning first, as a way of gaining some experience and getting a foot in the door."

"Wedding planner, huh? So what sparked off that dream? Was it because your parents had some big fancy wedding?"

Natalie looked out to sea. "Actually, my parents were never married."

"Oh."

Natalie shrugged. "It's no big deal, I guess—especially nowadays. There are lots of people whose parents never married." She glanced at him. "But maybe... yes... in a way that did play a part. I mean... I suppose I like the idea of giving couples the romantic fairy-tale ending that my own parents never had." She stopped speaking, feeling suddenly terribly vulnerable. She had never confessed her innermost motivations before. She had never really told anyone about these feelings—not even her grandmother—but there was something about Ben which made her want to open up for the first time in her life. In fact, it was almost a relief to talk about it at last.

"That's a worthy ambition," said Ben. "It's a shame, in a way, that your parents aren't here to see you achieve it."

"My father isn't dead."

Ben glanced at her. "Is he here in Summer Beach? Sorry—I don't mean to pry, but you did say before that you only had your grandmother. I just assumed that your parents were dead."

"No, he doesn't live here. He lives in the States. He's American."

Ben looked surprised. "Don't you keep in touch?"

Natalie turned her face away. "No."

Ben frowned. He seemed about to say something else, then changed his mind. They walked on again in silence. Finally, Ben cleared his throat and said:

"How did your parents meet if your father was American? Did he come and visit Australia?"

"No. He was a musician. A rock star, actually, and my mother was really into music—"

"A rock star! What's his name?"

"Jac Ludd."

"Jac Ludd?" Ben stopped walking and turned around to face her, his eyes widening incredulously. "You're Jac Ludd's daughter?"

Natalie shifted uncomfortably. "Yes." She turned around. "We should head back. I really need to get back to work."

She started off, but Ben put out a hand to stop her. "Wait... I know Ludd. He's a really decent guy. In fact, it was Ludd who helped me find my feet in the music industry. Without him, I wouldn't have the career I have today."

"Well, good for you," said Natalie tightly.

"Have you ever met him?"

Natalie shook her head.

"Well, then—how can you make any judgement about him? He must have tried to get in touch with you—"

"Yes, and I deleted all his messages unread and threw his cards in the bin," said Natalie shortly. "I'm not interested in anything he has to say."

"How do you know unless you read them?"

Natalie gave him an irritated look. "I don't care. Don't you see? I don't care what he has to say! I've never had a father in my life and I've done fine—why should I start involving him in my life now?"

Ben seemed about to say something then changed his mind.

Natalie sniffed. "In any case, I don't want to get involved with him and that whole lifestyle."

"There you go again: making assumptions," said Ben, with touch of impatience in his voice. "How do you know that he has any 'lifestyle' to speak of? You were completely wrong about me. Maybe you're wrong about him."

"I know I'm not. How else would my mother have ended up the way she did? Besides, Gran told me; she said Ludd was well known for his wild parties and drug habit and drinking and excesses."

"He may have been pretty wild twenty years ago, but he's mellowed a lot since. He is a changed man now. He isn't what you think he is at all, Natalie."

Natalie turned sharply away and started walking again. Ben hurried to catch up with her.

"Seriously, Natalie—why don't you give him a chance? He might have made mistakes when he was young... who hasn't? But he's done a lot of good in recent years. He donates to a lot of charities and uses his wealth and celebrity to help the underprivileged. If he's been reaching out to you—"

"Just drop it, okay?" said Natalie suddenly, swinging round to face him. "I don't want to talk about it anymore! I don't care if you know him, I don't care if he's the President of America! I just don't want to have anything to do with him, okay?"

Ben raised both hands in a placating gesture. "Okay." He reached out and touched her arm. "I'm sorry. I didn't mean to upset you."

Something in his voice brought sudden tears to Natalie's eyes. She blinked rapidly. "It's okay." She dashed the back of her hand across her eyes. "I know it's hard for people to understand, but he's never been in my life and I don't see any point in letting him in now."

"I hope that doesn't apply to other people," said Ben.

Natalie looked up at him. His dark hair was tousled by the sea breeze, and in the brilliant sunshine his eyes looked more green than grey. Something compelled her to take a step closer to him. They had come a long way up the beach and were alone here on the sand. Natalie felt her pulse begin to race as she read the intent in Ben's eyes. He reached out and pulled her to him, encircling her waist with his hands, and she came willingly, sliding her arms up around his neck.

"I think you're already a part of my life," said Natalie breathlessly.

"Good," murmured Ben, as he slowly lowered his head.

Natalie's heart pounded in her chest and she held her breath, her every sense waiting... waiting for that moment when his lips would touch hers. She had been yearning for this moment since yesterday. She wanted him to kiss her, to make her forget—

Rrrrrrring!

The shrill ringing of a mobile phone jarred Natalie out of the moment. Ben dropped his arms and stepped away from her as she looked around in confusion. She realised that the sound was coming from her own pocket. Fumbling, she pulled out her mobile and stared at the number. She didn't recognise it. Frowning, she put the phone to her ear.

"Hello—Natalie Walker speaking."

"This is the Central Coast Regional Hospital. My name's Pat Johnson. I'm one of the nurses in the Emergency Department. I just wanted to inform you that your grandmother has been brought in."

"Why? What's happened? Is she okay?" Natalie gripped the phone tight.

"She's had a bad fall, but she's stable now. She's just going in to have some X-rays. It might be a good idea for you to come as soon as you can."

"I'll leave right now. I should be there in twenty minutes."

"What's happened?" asked Ben as she put the phone down and tried to push it back into her pocket with trembling fingers.

"It's my grandmother. She's in hospital. They said she's had a fall and I—" Natalie covered her mouth suddenly and took a shuddering breath.

"Hey... Hey..." Ben put a reassuring arm around her shoulders. "Let's get to the hospital and find out more before we jump to conclusions, eh?"

"Oh, no, you don't have to—"

"I'm coming with you. Don't argue." Ben's voice was firm as he began steering her back up the beach towards the resort.

Natalie started to protest again, then closed her mouth. The truth was, she didn't want to face this alone. Ben's presence was incredibly reassuring. She wanted him with her.

She glanced down to where her hand was still held securely in his. Suddenly, she wasn't sure if she ever wanted him to let go.

CHAPTER FOURTEEN

Sara winced as the hairstylist shoved a pin into her hair and it grazed her scalp. She stared at her reflection in the mirror and reminded herself that vanity did not come without suffering. Still, her hair looked amazing and she couldn't wait to see how it would match her gown on the actual day.

"Sorry... didn't mean to stab you, but I need to make sure this is absolutely secure and won't come undone on the day, because it'll be really windy down on the beach." The hairstylist placed a cluster of silk flowers into Sara's hair and secured it with more hairpins. "I'm glad you're not going for a full veil, though. I've seen some disasters with that at beach weddings, where a gust of wind practically dragged the bride out to sea."

Sara giggled in spite of herself.

"What about the wedding programmes?" asked Ellie from the neighbouring chair where she was flicking through some magazines. "What if they start blowing around—"

"Natalie's thought of that already," says Sara. "She's having the programme printed on the back of some pretty paper fans and then they'll be handed out to the guests when they arrive. That way, they'll do double duty: people will be able to use them to keep cool and also have a souvenir of the wedding."

"Great idea." Ellie smiled. "Natalie's come up with some great stuff, hasn't she? I really liked her idea for the seahorse place-card holders as well."

"Yes, I'm so glad I got her on board."

"Not that it seems to have stopped you stressing," observed to Ellie dryly.

Sara gave a rueful smile. "I just—"

She broke off as the door to the salon opened and two people hovered uncertainly in the doorway. It was Jenn and the cameraman. They caught her eye in the mirror and gave her a wary smile.

"We heard that you'd be doing a trial run at the hairdressers so we thought maybe we could get some footage?" Jenn asked.

Sara sighed. "Sure, come in."

She noted the way they practically tiptoed into the salon and hovered nervously around her. She felt a bit bad. Craig must have really impressed upon them how annoyed she was after that last incident with the beach photos in the magazine.

Sara sighed again. She didn't want to have every aspect of her life under the spotlight, but she didn't like thinking everyone was scared of her and viewed her as some sort of Bridezilla either. She just wanted to enjoy her own wedding—was that too much to ask for? She wasn't like Ellie—needing to have everything perfect all the time—but she did so want to have things perfect for her special day.

The sound of her cell phone ringing interrupted her thoughts. Ellie leaned over, pulled the phone out of Sara's handbag, and looked at the screen. "It's an American number. California code, actually," she said frowning.

Sara looked at her in curiously. "Maybe it's one of our cousins who couldn't come to the wedding?"

"Maybe. I don't recognise the number though." Ellie handed the phone to Sara, who put it to her ear.

"Hello?"

"Sara! Baby, it's me. Jeff."

Sara stiffened. ""Jeff?" she croaked. She cleared her throat and tried again. "Jeff. How are you?"

"Awesome, baby, just awesome. I was calling to ask how you were."

"Me? I'm... I'm fine... In fact, I'm getting married in a few days," Sara said, slightly defiantly.

"Yeah, I heard that. I guess congratulations are in order—although I have to say, Sara, are you sure you know what you're doing?"

"What d'you mean?"

"Well... You know how good we were together, baby. I guess... with our history... I just wanted you to be sure that you're making the right decision."

"What does our history have anything to do with it?" Sara snapped. She glanced up and saw that Jenn and the cameraman were listening avidly, and the camera lens was trained on her. She made an effort to modulate her voice. "Yes, I am sure. I'm very happy with my decision."

"Oh, good. I just want you to be happy, baby. You know I just want you to be happy... That's why I've been thinking... I mean, as I said, we were so good together—it's crazy to throw that all away! I know there have been a few... er... issues and misunderstandings, maybe... but at the end of the day, all that matters is that we had something special together. What d'you say—we give it another try?"

"*What?*" Sara wasn't sure if she was hearing right. "You're the one who didn't appreciate the 'something special' we had," she said acidly.

"I know—and I was stupid." Jeff's voice was thick with remorse. "I have no defence. I'm sorry, baby, I was weak and that hussy completely took me in. She made me doubt my love for you. But since you've been gone, I've realised just how precious you are to me and how much I didn't value you. You're beautiful and wonderful and amazing, Sara! That was why I fell so head over heels in love with you when we met that day outside the supermarket.

I'm sick of all these fake, perfect Barbie dolls here in Hollywood—I should have realised my luck when I had a real woman like you in my arms." Jeff's voice trembled with emotion. "But baby... is it really over? Is there no chance for me to try and make amends? I know you must still care for me—you can't have forgotten all we had together! You're not seriously going to marry some Australian hick boy and spend the rest of your life in some godforsaken town Down Under? You belong here, in L.A. with me! Give me another chance, Sara, and I'll show you that I'm a man worthy of your love!"

For a tiny second, Sara wavered. Jeff's speech was pretty moving and his impassioned words did bring back all those heady moments when she had first met him and he had swept her off her feet. She had been a nobody—and he had made her feel like a princess, envied by every woman across America. And it had not been in spite of her fuller figure, but *because* of it. Jeff had broadcast everywhere that he had fallen for her because of her "real woman" curves and girl-next-door prettiness. It had been wonderfully flattering and empowering after years of anguish and insecurity about her looks and figure.

But those were lies, Sara reminded herself bitterly. Those had all been lies. Jeff hadn't meant any of those words. He had simply been using her: using her to boost his public image and present himself to the American public as some kind of gallant Prince Charming who valued women for their real selves... when all along, he had been cheating on her behind her back, with exactly the kind of glamorous, thin model he said he despised!

Oh God, she had been a fool. Jeff was an actor and he knew the right lines to say—and the right ways to say them. He knew how to conjure up sympathy and emotion. It was what he did for a living! He had lied before and he was still lying now... and she wasn't going to fall for it again. Craig was the real Prince Charming in her life: Craig, who didn't choose her because she was thin or curvy or tall or short—but simply because she was *her*; Craig, who didn't make a song and dance about anything, and yet loved her—the *real* her—with no judgement or reservations.

"You're good at pretty words, Jeff," Sara said at last into the phone. "But I learned the hard way a long time ago not to believe you. Did you really think I was going to come crawling back to you now? Yeah, you're right—you should have realised how lucky you were. Maybe you should have thought of that before you cheated on me with that bimbo!" The pain and humiliation of walking into Jeff's house and finding him in bed with the leggy blonde washed over Sara again. "When I think of how you embarrassed me in front of the whole nation... how people were laughing about me after we broke up and said that you ditched me because I was too fat... I can't believe I ever thought you loved me! So no, I'm not interested in your offer.

Goodbye!"

She stabbed the button on the phone to end the call. Then she raised her eyes and saw Craig in the mirror. He had obviously just come in and was standing stock still, watching her. She wondered how much of the conversation he had heard.

"Craig!" She whirled around in her chair.

"Who was that?" he asked, striding forwards.

"That was Jeff Kingston."

"What did that drongo want?" demanded Craig, his brows drawing together.

Sara hesitated, very aware of Jenn and the cameramen standing in the corner, their eyes goggling in their faces. The camera was obviously still rolling, recording everything that was happening. *What riveting TV this is going to be,* she thought bitterly. As if it wasn't bad enough that they were following her every move and highlighting her physical flaws for all to see, now they would be getting the scoop on all the private dramas as well!

Sara looked at Craig. "He heard about the wedding and wanted to send a friendly congratulation."

Craig frowned. "Didn't sound that friendly from what I heard of the call."

Sara shrugged. "He was just... getting a bit confused about things and I was setting him straight. Nothing to worry about."

"Who says I was worried?"

There was something in Craig's voice which

made Sara glance at him quickly. An unfamiliar tension rose between them and an awkward silence settled in the salon. Everyone seemed to be frozen, watching them.

Finally, Ellie cleared her throat and said, "So Craig, what d'you think of Sara's hair?"

Craig kept his eyes locked with Sara's for a moment longer, then he broke the gaze and turned away with a shrug. "Looks good. But then us blokes don't really notice these things."

"You don't notice—until it *doesn't* look good..." Sara muttered.

"Um... What about you, Craig?" asked the hairstylist quickly. "Do you want me to do something special with your hair on the day?"

Craig reeled back in horror. "Bloody hell, no! No one's touching my hair on the day but me, and all it's getting is a shampoo and a brush. I'm already wearing this linen suit and silk tie—that's more than fancy enough for me."

"Personally, I think you vets should get married in your scrubs," said Ellie with joking leer. "Nothing is as sexy as a man in tight-fitting scrubs. I've told Dan that if we ever get married, that's what I want him to wear. And a stethoscope and white coat for accessories!"

Ellie's comment eased the atmosphere a bit and everybody laughed nervously. Sara gave Craig a hesitant smile and told him about her idea for a Tim Tam cake.

"I spoke to Natalie this morning and she's going to speak to Jean-Pierre, the resort chef, about it. But she thinks it'll be okay—in fact, she thinks he might come up with something really special."

Craig smiled. "A Tim Tam cake, eh? That'll be a first. Well, whatever makes you happy is good enough for me."

He leaned over and kissed her on the forehead. Sara heard a happy sigh come from Jenn in the corner and knew that the moment had obviously been caught on film. She glanced quickly at Craig again, wondering if he was playing up to the cameras—then felt ashamed of her own thoughts. *Craig isn't like Jeff*, she reminded herself. He really meant it when he said that he wanted her to be happy.

This time she really had found Prince Charming and this story *was* going to have a happy ending.

CHAPTER FIFTEEN

Natalie chewed her fingernail and stared at the clock on the Emergency Department wall. Her grandmother had been in for over two hours now and she still hadn't heard any news. What was happening? What were they doing to her?

She chewed on her fingernail again, then caught herself as she realised what she was doing. Her grandmother's voice echoed in her ears. How many times had Gran told her off for biting her nails? The thought brought home to Natalie again how big a presence her grandmother was in her life and what a huge hole she would leave behind if she was gone.

Suddenly, all her fears came rushing back—all her thoughts from the other morning, when she had contemplated the frightening prospect of life without her grandmother in it. She couldn't bear the thought of it: to have no one nag her about her bad habits; no one give her a hug and soothe her when things went wrong; no one to encourage her to stand up again when she had fallen. Panic overwhelmed her.

"Hey..."

Her hand was suddenly caught in a strong, warm grasp and Ben gently drew her fingers away from her mouth.

"It's going to be okay, Natalie. I know your grandmother's had a nasty fall, but there was no bleeding. They just need to check to make sure she hasn't broken any bones."

"But what if they find something worse?" asked Natalie in a fearful whisper. "What if they find there's internal bleeding? Or she's ruptured something? Or—"

"Shh..." Ben reached out and rubbed her shoulders. "You're letting your imagination run away with you. I'm sure if it was really anything serious, she would have been in Intensive Care and not just waiting for an X-ray. She's probably just delayed because she's in a line waiting for her turn."

"Yes, there's always a bloody queue..." said Natalie bitterly. "Everything takes forever in the public system."

"At least you've *got* a public health system."

Natalie looked at him. "What do you mean?"

"Healthcare in the US is horrific. You pretty

much don't get treated unless you've got health insurance and that can get very expensive, especially if you're self-employed."

"You mean—if people have an emergency, they can't go to the hospital?"

Ben shrugged. "Oh, I guess they can go to the hospital, but then they'll get hit with a whopping bill afterwards. It's why there are so many people who have declared bankruptcy due to their medical bills."

"But... I don't understand... I mean, we have private health insurance in Australia too. Gran and I just can't afford it; that's why she's having to wait so long for this hip operation—if she had private health insurance, she could have gone to a private hospital and had the op ages ago."

"But when she *does* get the operation, the government pays for it all, right? You won't be getting a bill for the hospital stay and the surgeon's fees."

Natalie nodded. "That's what our taxes are for."

"Well, we pay taxes in the U.S. too, but unfortunately, it doesn't help much with healthcare. Seriously, you guys are lucky. You don't know what it's like not to have a proper public healthcare system. You might have to wait a bit longer, but at least you'll get taken care of eventually and you won't have to pay a cent."

Natalie digested this. She hadn't realised there was such a difference between the two countries and it did put things in perspective—it made her feel a bit better about the long wait her grandmother was having to endure. She was also surprised to find that she felt calmer now; somehow, the talk about healthcare systems had distracted her from her worries.

At that moment, the doors to the inner treatment area of the ED swung open and a young doctor stepped through. His eyes met Natalie's and he smiled as he came over.

"Natalie Walker?"

Natalie sprang up. "Yes, that's me! How's my Gran?"

"She's just had her X-rays. She's doing fine," the doctor reassured her. "It looks like she didn't break any bones, although she's had a bad ankle sprain."

"What happened to her?" asked Natalie.

"She says she fell down the stairs. She must have slipped and lost her footing." The doctor shook his head. "She's actually lucky that she didn't do anything more than sprain her ankle."

"What about her hip?" asked Natalie.

"So far as we can see, the hip doesn't seem to be injured. There might be some bruising, but overall she's been very fortunate. I see she's due to have her op in a couple of months. You might want to keep an eye on her until then, just to make sure she doesn't have any more falls like this."

Natalie looked at him in concern. "Why should she be more likely to fall?"

"It's the pain in her hip," the doctor explained. "She's got very arthritic hip joints and it causes a lot of swelling and pain on movement. We find that patients with these symptoms tend to take the weight off the painful hip when they walk. And when they do that, they can sometimes lose their balance, especially if there is uneven footing. It's pretty common in those with dodgy hips."

"Does she have to stay in hospital?" Natalie asked worriedly.

The doctor shook his head, smiling. "No, we're giving her some pain medication now, and then she'll be discharged and ready to go home. But she has to keep off that ankle for forty-eight hours until the swelling goes down. Best if she doesn't weight bear at all on both feet. I'll see if I can organise for you to borrow a wheelchair—"

"We wouldn't have the right access for it at home anyway," said Natalie regretfully. "We live in a two-storey cottage and it's pretty small."

The doctor frowned. "You've got stairs at home? Hmm... well, you might have to consider letting your grandmother sleep downstairs for a few nights. And you might need someone to help move her." He looked Natalie up and down. "Have you got a male relative—a brother or father—to help with lifting her and things?"

"No—" Natalie started to say, but Ben interrupted.

"I'd be happy to help."

Natalie turned and stared at him. "But..."

Ben nodded firmly. "I can come back home with you now and help settle her in."

"That would be the best," said the doctor. He turned to Natalie. "I can take you in to see her now if you like."

Natalie nodded eagerly and followed the doctor into the treatment area. They found her grandmother in a cubicle at the far end, with the curtains half drawn around her. Natalie felt relief wash over her as she saw that her grandmother was sitting up, propped by pillows. Rita's eyes lit up as she saw Natalie, then they widened with interest as they fell on Ben.

"Oh, Gran!" cried Natalie, running over to throw her arms around her grandmother and bury her face in the old woman's neck.

Rita patted her gently. "Hey, possum... What's this? Don't be silly! It was just a little fall!"

Natalie drew back, sniffing and wiping her eyes. "I was just so worried, Gran! I thought—" she gulped.

Rita patted her back and smiled. "My goodness, Natalie, when did you become such a sook? It was my own fault for being careless. The phone was ringing and I was hurrying downstairs to answer it. I must've missed a step. Lucky that I was almost at the bottom."

"Oh Gran, I *told* you—we've got an answering machine now! You can always ring people back if you've missed their call," said Natalie.

Rita gave a rueful smile. "Well, I've learned that lesson the hard way, haven't I?" She turned to look at Ben again. "And is this your American friend?"

"Oh, yeah... Gran, this is Ben. Ben Falco." Natalie stepped back to let Ben come forwards.

He bent and offered his hand to Rita. "Sorry it's under these circumstances, Mrs Walker, but I'm very pleased to meet you."

"Call me Rita—and I'm delighted to meet you at last, whatever the circumstances."

The doctor, who had been watching the conversation up till now, stepped in and explained about Ben's offer to help.

"But really... it's not necessary... we can't put Ben to that trouble—" Natalie started to protest again.

"That's very kind of you, young man," said Rita, looking at Ben approvingly. She glanced at Natalie's flushed face, then at him, then back to Natalie again. "I'd be very grateful to accept your offer."

Half an hour later, they were settled in the car and on the way home. Natalie felt slightly self-conscious at the thought of Ben seeing her house. She and her grandmother shared an old fisherman's cottage, with an extension added to the attic to convert it into two storeys. It was quaint and comfortable, but it certainly wasn't stylish or spacious.

When they arrived at the cottage, however, Ben

showed no disdain or even surprise at the humble accommodation. Instead, he admired the little front garden full of lily pilly and dog roses, and remarked on the cosiness of the cottage interior. He was so tall, though, it almost looked as if he would have to stoop to enter, and once inside he seemed to dominate the room.

They busied themselves settling her grandmother in the living room with her injured leg propped up on a footstool. Then Natalie went into the kitchen to make everyone a cup of tea. Ben followed her a moment later and stood with his arms crossed, leaning against the doorjamb. He watched her as she filled the kettle and arranged the teabags in the mugs. His presence was distracting and Natalie found it hard to keep her mind on what she was doing—she almost added salt instead of sugar to the tea!

"What will you do at bedtime?" asked Ben.

Natalie furrowed her brow. "I don't know. I suppose I could try make up a bed for Gran in the living room. As you can see, there isn't much room downstairs. I'm not sure how comfortable she'll be on the settee. We do have a sleeping bag, but I can't ask Gran to sleep on the floor. The hard surface and draughts would be terrible for her arthritis."

"Why not just let her sleep in her own bed? I'm sure she would sleep much better there and it's important she has a good rest."

"I'd love to, but how am I going to get her up

those stairs?"

"I could help. If your grandmother doesn't mind, I could carry her easily up the stairs."

"Yes, but... I don't think it would be very fair to her. It wouldn't be nice to put her there now and leave her upstairs all evening. Besides, there's no TV in her room—"

"Oh, I didn't mean now. I meant much later—when she's ready for bed."

Natalie looked at him in surprise. "But that would mean that you'd have to..."

"Stay the night? I don't mind. I'm perfectly happy in a sleeping bag—it wouldn't be the first time."

"I can't ask you to hang around here all evening just to help my grandmother tonight—"

"Why not? And you're not asking. I'm offering. I *want* to stay and help. Besides..." He pushed away from the doorjamb and came towards her. "It would give me a chance to spend more time with you."

Natalie dropped her gaze, unable to meet his eyes. "Well... Um... I guess, I could ask Gran if she's happy with the idea..."

She darted around him and practically ran out of the kitchen. She didn't know why she had run away like that, but suddenly, she felt overwhelmed by how things were progressing between her and Ben. He liked her—he was making it obvious—but what did she feel about him? Did she really want this to go anywhere? *Could* it go anywhere?

She recalled Ben's words on their hike: *"I think I*

might have a reason to come back." She felt herself blush and hoped that her grandmother wouldn't notice as she walked back into the living room.

Rita Walker was delighted with Ben's offer and quick to accept, although Natalie wasn't sure if her grandmother's alacrity was for her own sake or her granddaughter's. She certainly caught a shrewd look in her grandmother's eyes as Ben came back out from the kitchen and joined them.

Natalie felt her heart flutter as she thought of Ben passing the night in the cottage. A part of her was thrilled at the chance to spend so much more time with him, to get to know him even better—but there was another part which was restless and uneasy, though she could not understand why.

CHAPTER SIXTEEN

Ben looked across the living room at Natalie. She was curled up at the other end of the couch, her attention riveted on the TV screen, her chin in one hand. She was dressed in a simple sweater and faded jeans, and her face was scrubbed free of make-up, making her look much younger. Ben felt something powerful stir in his chest and had to resist the urge to reach for her.

It had been the most wonderful evening he had spent in a long time. Not that they had done anything particularly special: they had watched some TV, talked a bit, then had a simple meal rustled up by Natalie in the small cottage kitchen. Afterwards, they'd played a board game and laughed as they discussed some more differences between Australia and the U.S.

He couldn't remember the last time he had felt so relaxed and welcomed and "part of a family". Although he had only met Rita for the first time today, somehow he felt like he had known her for years. And as for Natalie herself, it was as if he had discovered a very precious part of him that had always been missing, but he had never realised... until he met her.

Rita yawned and stretched next to him. "Well... I think I'm going to head upstairs. I'm not sure if I'll sleep just yet—I think I might read in bed for a while."

"Let me know when you're ready for bed, Gran, and I'll come and help you in the bathroom," said Natalie.

Her grandmother nodded. "And don't worry about me—I can't hear anything when my bedroom door's shut so if you want to watch TV or something, it won't disturb me."

Ben got up and carefully lifted Rita in his arms.

"I think the last time I was carried like this, I was a new bride," Rita laughed. She winked at Natalie. "Your grandfather was old-fashioned. He insisted on carrying me over the threshold of the cottage, but he did his back in so badly, he never tried to carry me again!" She looked at Ben. "I hope this won't hurt your back—"

Ben shook his head, chuckling. "You should see some of the heavy sound equipment I've had to move in my time. You're a featherweight compared to that."

He carried her carefully up the stairs and into her bedroom. He settled her on the bed and made sure she had everything within easy reach, then turned to leave. But as he was about to step out the door, he paused as he spied something in the corner of the room.

It was a guitar, he realised. A beautiful vintage Gibson with a rosewood fingerboard and Kluson-style gold tuners. Drawn by the beauty of the instrument, he moved towards it and reached out a hand to stroke the spruce wood finish.

"It was Natalie's mother's."

Ben turned to see Rita looking sadly at the guitar. "She loved music, my Annabel. She used to play and sing all the time—she had a wonderful voice."

"Natalie has an amazing voice too," said Ben.

Rita looked at him in surprise. "You've heard her sing?"

"Only once. The first time I met her. We were in the car on the way back from the hospital and I started singing along to a song on the radio—and she joined in. But I got the feeling that she forgot herself for a moment."

Rita sighed. "Yes. That's why I was surprised. I haven't heard her sing in years. She won't let herself. It's like... it's like she censors herself." She looked at him, her eyes filled with sadness. "It's heartbreaking, because she has such a beautiful voice. When she was a little girl, she used to sing with her mother—they would sit out in the garden on a summer night and sing together. It's one of the most beautiful memories I have of Annabel." She sighed again and said wistfully, "I would love to hear Natalie sing again."

Rita grabbed a tissue suddenly from the table next to her bed and dabbed her eyes.

Ben made a movement towards her. "I'm sorry. I didn't mean—"

"No, no..." Rita waved her hand. "I'm fine. To be honest with you, it feels good to mention Annabel, to talk about her. In recent years, Natalie has become completely irrational on the subject of her mother. She refuses to talk about her or do anything that brings up her memory. It's almost as if she wants to pretend that her mother doesn't exist!"

"Maybe the thought of her mother brings back painful memories and so she wants to avoid that," Ben suggested.

"No, it's not that. It's more that she's afraid."

"Afraid?" Ben frowned. "What's Natalie afraid of?"

Rita hesitated. "She's afraid of becoming like her mother."

"Why should she be afraid of that?"

Rita sighed. "Annabel was a bit of a wild child. I guess she was what people would call 'a free spirit'. When she was sixteen, she fell madly in love with an American rock star called Jac Ludd. She decided that she just couldn't be happy unless she was with him—even though he didn't even know she existed. So she saved up and bought a one-way ticket to the U.S. We woke up one morning and she was gone. It nearly killed my husband, I can tell you. Annabel was an only child and he was very protective of her. As I said, he was old-fashioned and he had very conservative ideas. He just couldn't understand Annabel and her need for creative expression, her need to be free. They were constantly arguing, constantly fighting over her music, her clothes, her friends... but when she was gone, it was like she took a part of him with her."

"Didn't Annabel ever come back?"

"Oh, she did. Especially when things got tough and the money ran out. She'd come back for a bit... but in a few months, she'd be off again. I don't know if it was just Ludd or the glamorous world that he represented. Annabel had always been very musical and I guess she was desperate to be part of that scene, I don't know... maybe even make her own dreams of a musical career come true." Rita's mouth twisted. "Instead, what actually happened was that she fell in with the wrong crowd. She became one of Ludd's groupies and joined the whole wild lifestyle—the drugs, the drinking, the crazy parties... I pleaded with her to come back to Summer Beach, but she wouldn't listen."

Rita sat up straighter. "Then one day, she did come back—and she had a baby with her. It was

Natalie. Annabel said the baby was Ludd's child—but to be honest, even if she hadn't told me, I would have guessed. You only had to look at the baby: she had his chin, his eyes..." She sighed. "I thought maybe now that she had a baby, Annabel would finally settle down, but the lure of her life in America was just too much for her. She was soon off again, leaving the baby with us. Of course, my husband was delighted. It was as if someone had given him Annabel back again. He doted on Natalie, although sadly he died when she was just two years old. Lung cancer," Rita added at Ben's enquiring look. "He was a terrible smoker."

"So it was just you and Natalie after that?"

Rita nodded. "Oh, Annabel still came back occasionally, breezing in and out of our lives—and when she was around, everything would be wonderful for a while. She was always laughing and singing and the house was filled with music. Natalie absolutely worshipped her. But the visits got more and more infrequent. And after a while, I could see how the lifestyle was taking its toll on my beautiful daughter. I was shocked to see how ill she looked whenever she came back. Well, the lifestyle caught up with her when Natalie was eight years old. Annabel died of a drug overdose."

Ben felt his heart squeeze inside him as he thought of the young Natalie losing her mother like that. He had seen his fair share of drug abuse and alcohol addiction by now—it was almost unavoidable when you moved in the circles he did—but it still didn't make each death easier to accept.

Rita took a deep breath. "I think Natalie blamed her father for taking her mother away from her. She never knew him—she just knew that he was the reason her mother went away every time and the reason why her mother never came back again one day. As she grew older, she also developed this terrible fear of becoming like her mother. She saw Annabel as an out-of-control drug addict who left her only child and ran off to be someone's groupie. She's terrified that it will be her own fate too if she's not careful." She shook her head. "I keep trying to tell Natalie that she's a completely different person from her mother—she really *is* nothing like Annabel—but I don't think Natalie believes it. She adored her mother, but when Annabel died, she was absolutely devastated, and somehow all her hero worship turned into bitterness. She stopped talking about her, stopped responding when we mentioned Annabel."

"And her father?"

Rita shook her head in exasperation. "Jac Ludd has been trying really hard, but Natalie rejects all his attempts to make contact. He sent her letters and cards and emails and even tried to call. She refused them all. He still keeps trying—after all these years, he still sends a card regularly, but she won't open them, no matter how much I urge her to."

Ben said slowly, "I know Ludd. He is a sort of a mentor, you could say. I know he had a wild reputation when he was younger, but he's changed a lot in recent years. He's like a different man now."

"Yes, that's what I've heard. And actually, he has always been very kind to me. He only found out about Natalie after Annabel's death and he contacted me immediately, asking if he could help to support her in any way. I didn't really like to take his money, although I've let him help with the odd Christmas present or school trip or other special treat. When Natalie got old enough and found out, she blankly refused to take anything from him, but I've kept in touch with him over the years. I send him the occasional photo or update when I can." She sighed. "I know he would love to meet her—and I *want* him to. It's wrong that Natalie doesn't know her father at all. But I can't get through to her and I don't know if it'll ever happen."

She gestured to the guitar. "You can take it and try it if you like. It would be nice, actually, to hear the sound of music in this house again."

"Are you sure?"

"Yes."

Ben picked up the guitar carefully. It was covered in dust, but when he blew on it gently, the polished mahogany showed a beautiful rich brown in the soft lamplight.

"I'll take it downstairs and try it out," he said. "And thank you. For telling me everything."

"I think it's time Natalie started tearing down the walls she's built around herself." Rita looked him straight in the eye. "And I think you might be the one to help her."

CHAPTER SEVENTEEN

Natalie was in the kitchen, washing up, when she heard Ben come downstairs again. He had been quite a while upstairs—she wondered what he had been doing. Probably chatting to her grandmother. She hoped Gran hadn't been sharing embarrassing childhood stories.

She rinsed the last plate and stacked it on the dish rack, then dried her hands on a tea towel. She was suddenly eager to get back to Ben; it was embarrassing to admit it, but she had almost missed him in the short time he had been upstairs.

As she stepped into the living room, however, Natalie froze. Ben was sitting on the edge of settee, and balanced on one knee was a guitar.

Her mother's guitar.

She gripped the side of the doorjamb. Ben hadn't

noticed her yet—he was softly strumming the guitar and humming under his breath, pausing every so often to adjust the tuning pegs. Natalie felt her heart hammering in her chest as her breath came fast and shallow.

Ben looked up and saw her. "Hey..." He smiled and patted the seat on the couch next to him.

"Where did you get that?" Natalie whispered.

"It's your mother's."

"I know."

"Your grandmother gave it to me. She said I could play it." Ben looked at her in concern. "Natalie? Are you okay? I didn't mean to upset you."

She licked dry lips and took a deep breath. "No. It's okay... it was just a bit of a shock..." She came slowly over and sat down next to him. "I... I haven't seen anyone play that guitar in a long time."

Ben offered her the instrument. "Do you play?"

Natalie hesitated. "Not for a long time."

"Wanna try?"

She looked at it longingly, then shook her head and turned away. "No, thanks."

Ben regarded her for a moment, then said easily, "Okay, what would you like me to play, then? Any requests?"

Natalie opened her mouth to say "No", but to her surprise, what came out of her mouth instead was: "'Could I Have This Kiss Forever'. It was my mother's favourite song. She used to sing it all the time—and get me to sing it with her."

"Yeah, it's a duet," Ben agreed. "Wanna try it with me?"

Natalie stiffened.

"Okay, how about another song then," said Ben hastily.

"She also liked 'Smoke On The Water'. She used to play that a lot."

Ben smiled, then bent his head over the guitar and began to play. Natalie held her breath as the music washed over her. Every memory of her mother came rushing back in a flood of emotion. She hadn't allowed herself to even *think* of Annabel Walker for so long and now suddenly it was as if her mother had been given back to her.

When the last note had died away, Ben looked up and met her eyes. He put the guitar down carefully and moved closer to her. Reaching out, he gently wiped the tears from her eyes with his fingers. Then he leaned close and pressed his lips where his fingers had been.

Natalie gasped softly. Ben moved his lips to her temple, then traced a lingering path down along her jawline until he came to the corner of her mouth. He paused for a second and Natalie felt as if every cell in her body was straining towards him, waiting for the next moment... then his mouth was on hers, hot and demanding, kissing her with a passion that made her feel as if she was drowning in a maelstrom of emotions.

She made a soft whimper at the back of her

throat and slid her arms up around his neck. Ben's arms came around her, crushing her to his body. He kissed her with a fierceness that was almost frightening, his mouth moving across hers possessively, claiming her as his. It was thrilling, it was exhilarating, it was the most incredible feeling she had ever experienced and she never wanted that moment to end.

"Good morning."

Natalie looked up from the cafetière. Her heart flipped over at the sight of Ben with his dark hair sleep-tousled and his clothes slightly rumpled. He looked adorable and sexy at the same time.

"I'm sorry—did I wake you? I was trying to be quiet but—"

"No, no... I was drifting awake anyway. I'm usually an early riser." He sniffed appreciatively. "That smells good."

"I'm making coffee. Want some?"

"Thanks. How did your grandmother sleep?"

"I'm just taking some coffee up to her now so I'll find out." She glanced at him from underneath her eyelashes. After the kiss between them last night, she felt as if she ought to be shy with Ben. Instead, she was surprised by how easy and comfortable she felt with him. "Help yourself to toast or cereal or anything else you want in the fridge or pantry. I'll be down again as soon as I can. In fact, why don't you try some Vegemite on toast?"

"What's Vegemite?"

Natalie grinned and handed him a small jar filled with a dark substance. "The best Aussie invention in the world. Or the worst. See what you think."

She turned and went upstairs. She found her grandmother already sitting up in bed and could see that Rita had obviously washed and dressed.

"Gran! You didn't get out of bed by yourself?"

"Oh, don't get your knickers in a twist. I can't have you waiting on me every moment. I can manage a bit of hopping from the bed to the loo. I promise I kept the weight off my bad leg."

"What if you fall again?"

"Well, the floor's carpeted here so it'll cushion my landing..."

Natalie rolled her eyes and set her grandmother's mug down on the bedside table, then sat down at the foot of the bed. "You're terrible! What's the point of me and Ben making so much effort to—"

"How is Ben? Did he sleep all right?"

"Yes, I think so."

Rita smiled at her. "He's a nice boy."

Natalie blushed. "Yes, I think so too."

"So do you think there's any chance—?"

"Oh, Gran...!" Natalie heaved a sigh. "Even if we... well, how could there ever be a future for us? I mean, he's American and he lives in the States... and I live here in Summer Be—"

"You don't always have to live here."

Natalie stared at her. "What do you mean?"

"I mean you could go to America." Rita held her hand up. "And before you start, that does *not* mean you'll end up like your mother."

"No, I wasn't thinking that," said Natalie.

"No?" Rita raised her eyebrows in surprise.

Natalie looked down and fidgeted with a fold of the blanket. "I... I don't know... last night, when Ben played Mum's song on the guitar... it made me remember her. But in a good way. And I thought... well, maybe it's not so awful if I *am* a bit like her. Not the drugs and groupie part, of course," she said hastily. "But... there were other sides to her too."

Rita looked as if she was about to cry. "Thank God. At last," she whispered. She leaned forwards and caught Natalie's hand. "I can't tell you how happy I am to hear that."

Natalie gave her grandmother's hand a squeeze and smiled at her.

Rita sat back briskly. "And going back to what we were saying, there's nothing to stop you going to the States if things with Ben—"

"But I can't, Gran. I'd have to leave you alone here and I couldn't do that."

Rita smiled. "Well, actually... I've been waiting for the right moment to tell you, possum. I guess now is as good as any."

Natalie looked at her quizzically.

"I wouldn't be alone," said Rita. "You see, I've been enjoying a... er... special friendship with

Graham. And we've been talking about moving in together."

Natalie stared at her grandmother, open-mouthed. "Graham? Graham the postie?"

Rita nodded.

"You and Graham have been seeing each other all this time?"

"Well, it didn't start out romantic. We were really just friends—you know, a bit of bowls, a meal together afterwards, a night out at the cinema... but I guess it's grown into something more." She laughed at Natalie's expression. "Older people can have romances too, you know."

Natalie laughed as well. "Sorry... I just... Gran, that's wonderful! I'm really happy for you. Graham is a wonderful bloke."

Rita nodded. "He is. So you don't have to worry about going off and leaving me alone. I mean, I'm not encouraging you to leave or anything," she chuckled. "But don't let the thought of me stop you. I'll be fine."

Natalie leaned forwards and gave her grandmother a hug.

"And speaking of Graham, I rang him this morning and told him what happened. He's coming over as soon as his rounds are finished. So you can tell Ben that he can have a break from lifting duties. He'd probably like to get back to the resort."

"I'll go and let him know now," said Natalie, standing up. "And I'll ring the resort admin as well and ask for a day off, so I can stay and look after you."

"But what about the wedding? Don't you have lots of things to—"

"I've got most of the things under control. I can make a few calls from here, but otherwise everything is pretty much set for the wedding rehearsal tomorrow." Natalie bent down to drop a kiss on her grandmother's cheek. "Don't worry, Gran. I can spare the time. And I'll call Sara and let her know as well, in case she wants to reach me for something."

Natalie left her grandmother's room and ran down the stairs. For some reason, she was suddenly feeling particularly light-hearted and carefree. She told herself that it was because she was happy for her grandmother, but she knew, deep inside, that it was really because suddenly, there was a real chance for her and Ben to be together.

CHAPTER EIGHTEEN

The majestic strains of Pachelbel's 'Canon in D' filled the air as Sara laid her hand on her father's arm and they began their slow walk down the sandy aisle. Dan, the best man, and Pippa, one of the bridesmaids, walked ahead of them as they all headed towards the wedding canopy which stood by the edge of the water. It was not fully decorated yet—Natalie had attached the soft organza drapes and silk ribbons to the posts, but the fresh flowers would be added just before the ceremony tomorrow, so that they wouldn't wilt in the sun. Still, it was already a beautiful sight and Sara felt a jolt of excitement at the thought of standing under it with Craig for real.

She reminded herself to walk a bit slower, as she'd be wearing her gown tomorrow and not the current shirt dress. Her train would probably drag in the sand and weigh her down and, in any case, she wanted to make a slow, graceful entrance.

She'd felt a bit silly doing a rehearsal for such a small event. It wasn't as if they were having some grand wedding with a huge procession. This was meant to be a casual affair. But Natalie had insisted that a beach wedding always required a bit more planning and with so many guests coming from overseas, it was important to have everything go smoothly on the day.

Anyway, at least this wasn't like a traditional wedding rehearsal in the U.S. with the formal rehearsal dinner. Well, Craig *had* hosted a dinner for close friends and family at his place last night, but it was done in typical informal Aussie-style: beer and barbecue and everyone helping themselves!

Sara reached the end of the aisle and her father handed her over to Craig, who looked slightly incongruous in his T-shirt and jeans. He wasn't the only one. Most of the other men standing around them were in similarly summery clothes. It was turning out to be one of the warmest days they'd had so far this month and, with the sun blazing in the sky, it was hard to believe that this was supposed to be the middle of winter in Australia.

"Hope it's not this hot tomorrow," muttered Craig under his breath. "Can't imagine standing here in a suit and tie in this heat."

Sara smiled wryly to herself. She had never realised how much Aussie men hated dressing up. There had been a comical amount of grumbling from Craig and his friends since they learned of the dress code for the wedding. But at least the women would be pleased. From what she had seen, Australian women found the casual dress habits of their nation quite frustrating sometimes and relished the chance to be able to dress up and look fashionable and glamorous.

"Shhh! No talking," hissed Natalie, from where she was standing next to the canopy. "This is supposed to be like the real thing!"

"But we're not going to go through the whole ceremony, are we?" said Craig.

"I guess not," admitted Natalie. "I suppose you can have a read through of the ceremony in private. Okay, let's just pretend that it's done and you've kissed the bride... then you'll turn around and head back up the aisle... everyone just has to remember the order for the recession. Don't forget that Charlie isn't here today because she's on duty at the animal hospital, but we'll have one more bridesmaid tomorrow so that will slow things down a bit more."

Sara and Craig nodded.

"Okay, so the wedding party will follow you... Dan and Ellie as best man and maid of honour, then the bridesmaids, Pippa and Charlie... then your parents... and you'll lead the way to the reception area... over there." Natalie pointed to the pavilion tent that had been erected on the beachfront, just in front of the resort's gourmet restaurant.

Sara nodded again. "Got it." She hesitated, then added, "I hate to say this now, but... do you think that music is quite right?"

"I was thinking the same thing," said Craig. "Feels a bit too formal..."

"Pachelbel's 'Canon in D'?" said Natalie. "But we discussed this and you said that was what you wanted for walking down the aisle."

"I know," said Sara apologetically. "I know that was what I said. I guess it was the music I always associated with weddings. But hearing it now, it seems a bit wrong..."

Craig nodded. "Yeah. Feels like we need something with a bit more of a relaxed vibe."

"How about the Israel Kamakawiwo'ole version of 'Somewhere Over the Rainbow'?" Ben spoke up from where he was standing by the sound system. "He's a Hawaiian musician and his cover is one of the most popular and loved versions. The ukulele medley gives it a real tropical beachy vibe."

"Yes! I love that song," said Sara, beaming. "And that version is beautiful. It would be *perfect* for a beach wedding. Can you find it in time for tomorrow?"

"No worries, as you guys would say." Ben smiled.

"Cheers, mate." Craig smiled back at him.

Sara turned back to Natalie. "Okay. Shall we do

the rest of the—"

"Wait, what about Coco?" Natalie asked.

"Oh, God, yes, I'd totally forgotten about her!" Sara gasped. "Yes, we'd better practice the bit in the ceremony where she comes up the aisle with the rings..."

"Where is she?"

Sara looked around the beach area. "I don't know... Ellie was supposed to bring her and Milo... She's looking after the dogs today, although that pet sitter will be here tomorrow because Ellie's the maid of honour." She rolled her eyes. "I hope they'll be able to handle Milo—"

"It's a shame Dan can't look after the dogs because then they'd be perfectly behaved," said Craig, chuckling.

"Just stick a couple of liver treats in your pocket," Dan said with a grin. "You'll have no trouble getting the dogs to make a beeline for you down the aisle."

Sara laughed. Dan—Dr Dan O'Brien—was Craig's colleague at the Summer Beach Animal Hospital and a great friend. His deceptively easy-going demeanour hid a powerful, commanding presence and he was renowned for his ability to stay cool under pressure. He was the vet they always called when they had a particularly unruly or aggressive animal and he was also Ellie's boyfriend—although the jury was still out on whether he had managed to tame her strong-minded cousin!

Thoughts of her cousin made Sara looked around the beach again. Where *was* Ellie? Then she saw her. Ellie was standing at the back of the cordoned-off area, a leash in each hand, a Beagle and Labrador at her side. But Ellie's attention wasn't on the proceedings—she was standing next to Mrs Monroe and Aunt Sophie, and the three of them had their heads bent over something. Even from this distance, Sara could see the angry set of Ellie's shoulders. She felt a sense of foreboding.

Excusing herself, Sara hurried over to them. As she got closer, she saw that they were huddled over Ellie's cell phone.

"What's going on?"

The three of them started guiltily and looked up. Sara saw the dismay in her mother's eyes and reached for the phone. "What are you guys looking at?"

"Oh, it's just some dumb article," said Ellie quickly, shoving the phone back into her pocket.

"Let me see." Sara held out her hand "Come on, I promise I won't fly off the handle. I'm getting pretty used to the photos they're printing of me. What is it this time? Me coming out of the house with a huge zit on my face?"

"Er... This is a bit different," said Ellie.

Sara turned to her mother and her aunt. "What is it?"

They both looked uncomfortable.

"Honey, it's really not worth you bothering about," said Mrs Monroe. "You know they'll write anything these days to get a story. Your real friends won't believe—"

"Will somebody please tell me what you're all talking about or I'll scream!" said Sara in frustration.

Ellie sighed, then pulled her phone back out of her pocket and handed it over.

Sara looked down at the screen. It showed a piece on a celebrity news website, featuring an interview with Jeff Kingston.

Someone who has been very vocal this week on social media is actor Jeff Kingston, whose comments about his ex-girlfriend's upcoming wedding to Australian TV celebrity, Dr Craig Murray, has left the internet buzzing with speculation. During an exclusive interview, Kingston insisted that there were no hard feelings on his side.

"I wish her all the best, of course," he said. "Although I think it's sad when people feel the need to prove a point like this. I did contact Sara—just to offer her my congratulations—and it was obvious that she still hasn't gotten over me. But she's just too proud to admit it. I mean, look at her shacking up with some second-rate celebrity from Down Under. She must miss all the media attention she used to enjoy as my girlfriend and she's hoping to get some paparazzi love again. In fact, she even hinted to me

that she'd hoped I might be willing to give us another chance—I think she was really disappointed when I told her that chapter was closed in my life."

Cynics have suggested that Kingston's sudden loquacity on the subject was prompted by a recent drop in the ratings of his TV show, Rogue Protector, *and the rumours that it was to be axed. Since his interview, however, ratings have jumped again and his public profile has been the highest since the early days of his much-publicised romance with Sara Monroe.*

Sara felt her blood boiling. "The arrogant, lying, no-good son of a..." she spluttered.

"He's a jerk, we knew that," said Ellie. "Or as the Aussies would say, he's flaming galah. I swear, the Aussies have much better insults. Anyway, don't waste your energy on him, coz. Seriously, he's not worth—"

"I can't believe he said that about me!" Sara seethed. "*He* was the one who asked if we could get back together, not me! How *dare* he! The whole thing's a blatant lie! *He* was the one who was disappointed. *He* was the one who—"

"What's going on?" Craig had joined them and was looking at them curiously.

In answer, Sara handed the phone to him and Craig read the article. His lips tightened in anger.

"Who says I haven't gotten over him? The lying bastard! What does he mean I'm trying to prove a point?" Sara stormed, clenching her fists. "I *never* liked the media attention—that was the *worst* part of being his girlfriend—but he's making me sound like some desperate, pathetic—"

"You've got to calm down and not let him get to you," said Ellie.

"Easy for you to say!" snapped Sara.

"Ellie is right," said Craig. "I don't understand why you're getting so worked up about this."

"So worked up?" Sara said shrilly. Everybody on the beach turned to look at her. She flushed. "Of course I'm getting worked up! Who wouldn't get worked up? Did you read what he said about me? About you? Did you see the bit where he called you a second-rate—"

"I read it," said Craig evenly. "But you know it's not true. And people who really know us will know it's all a load of crock. Why is it bothering you so much?"

Sara glared at him. "I can't believe you don't understand this."

Craig's voice had an uncharacteristic edge. "What I don't understand is why you care so much."

Sara saw Ellie and the others eye them both nervously, then move discreetly away, leaving them alone.

"He's humiliating us!" Sara hissed at Craig. "How can you just stand there and accept that?"

"I don't accept it," said Craig impatiently. "But what are we going to do about it? He's thousands of miles away on the other side of the ocean and we're here. Our wedding is tomorrow. Are you really going to let this ratbag spoil everything? You're getting yourself so worked up—it's as if you still care so much about what he thinks. Is that what it is? That you still care?"

Sara looked at him wildly. "Of course not!" she snapped. "I can't believe you would even think that."

"Well, I don't know what to think," said Craig grimly. "Ever since this whole wedding thing started, you've just been getting more and more stressed and more and more unlike yourself. I don't know what's happened to the woman I fell in love with! And every single time you've been the most upset, it's been to do with your ex-boyfriend. Makes me wonder if you really are happy about this whole thing... whether you really want to marry me."

Sara gasped. From the corner of her eye, she could see that several of the others had also heard Craig's statement and everyone was looking worried.

Dan came towards them and put a hand on Craig's shoulders. "Whoa... time for a bit of a timeout, I think."

Ellie hurried over as well and grabbed Sara's arm. "Yeah, come on. Why don't we go get a drink? I think the rehearsal's probably done for the day. I'm sure we can muddle through it somehow tomorrow."

Sara stared at her cousin in amazement. She had never known Ellie to suggest to "muddle through" anything! In fact, she had expected Ellie to want them to rehearse the whole thing multiple times until they could perform it with military precision.

"We'll just practice calling Coco up the aisle," Ellie suggested, pulling Sara towards the canopy. "But we don't need the guys for that." She gave Dan a significant look.

He took the hint. "Yeah, why don't we go and have a beer, mate? It's getting bloody hot here." He led Craig away.

Sara shrugged off Ellie's hand. "I don't know why we're bothering," she muttered. "Maybe there won't even *be* a wedding tomorrow."

Ellie exchanged a look of alarm with Mrs Monroe and said with a weak laugh, "Don't be silly. Everyone's just getting a bit stressed out, that's all. Come on—I know the dogs always cheer you up. Let's go and run things through with them, okay?"

Sara gave Craig's retreating back one last look, then she nodded miserably and followed her cousin back to the wedding canopy.

CHAPTER NINETEEN

Natalie had watched the argument between Craig and Sara from the other side of the beach with troubled eyes. She hadn't felt it was in her place to interfere, as she didn't know them that well and, in any case, Dan and Ellie seemed to have got the situation in hand. Hopefully, once they had had a chance to cool off, the wedding couple would kiss and make-up.

Natalie sighed. This wasn't how she imagined the wedding rehearsal would go and now she was worried about tomorrow. Surely there wasn't any serious intent to call off the wedding? She had always imagined that planning a wedding for a couple who were as in love as Craig and Sara would be the most wonderful, rewarding experience. But so far the whole lead-up had been fraught with unexpected tensions and stresses. She had seen Sara become slowly and slowly more emotional and volatile, whilst even Craig's easy-going patience was giving way. And now the wedding rehearsal had ended with the couple fighting. This wasn't the day she had been expecting.

And then there was Ben...

Natalie threw a troubled look over to where Ben was standing by the sound system. She hadn't seen him since yesterday morning when he had left the cottage and gone back to the resort. She had wanted to call him last night, but had stopped herself, not wanting to come across too pushy or needy. She had been a bit surprised that *he* hadn't rung, but she'd told herself that he was probably busy sorting out things with the band and rehearsing for the performance tomorrow night.

Besides, Natalie knew that she would see him at the rehearsal today and she had been counting the minutes. She remembered the ease and closeness between them at the cottage and she couldn't wait to see Ben again; to feel the warmth of his smile, the tenderness in his gaze...

Ben had kept a mostly low profile during the rehearsal but she had sensed something different about him from the moment he arrived. He had seemed tense and awkward, and wouldn't quite meet her eyes. She was surprised and confused by his sudden withdrawal.

Was he regretting what had happened at the

cottage that night? Was he regretting that kiss?

The thoughts had tormented Natalie throughout the rehearsal and they returned with force now. She looked at Ben again, then took a deep breath and walked over to him.

"Hi..." She smiled at him.

He returned her smile absently. "Hi..." He nodded in Sara's direction. "I hope that wasn't anything serious."

"Me too," said Natalie. "I can't believe they're actually fighting. I have never seen them even argue. They always seem so happy and in love..."

"Even those really in love can clash over different beliefs about things," said Ben.

"What do you mean?"

Ben hesitated, then shrugged and said, "Nothing."

Natalie stiffened. "You're thinking of my father again, aren't you?" She heaved a sigh of exasperation. "I told you the other day—I'm not interested in him."

"How can you not be interested? He's your father."

"I don't think of him as my father. He's just a man I happen to share some DNA with. He's nothing else to me."

"That's because you've never give him a chance," Ben muttered.

"Why should I?" Natalie snapped. "Look what he did to my mother! Why should I have anything to do with the man who helped destroy her?"

"Your mother had to take some responsibility for her own fate. She made the decisions, whatever the influences might have been. She was an adult. Nobody forced her to choose that path," Ben retorted. "And people do make mistakes. People change. Besides, you shouldn't judge others based on their relationships with someone else—"

"Why shouldn't I?" demanded Natalie. "How else am I supposed to judge them?"

"By their interactions with you!" said Ben. He ran a frustrated hand through his hair. "You've never had a direct conversation with your father; you've never even let yourself hear what he has to say! Maybe if you gave him the chance—see what he actually has to say—before jumping to conclusions—"

"I don't see why this matters to you," said Natalie. "It's my father and my business."

"You're right, I'm sorry," said Ben quietly. He took a deep breath and let it out again. "Look, I don't want us to fight about this. All I'm saying is that maybe you could try to keep a more open mind about it, that's all."

Natalie took a deep breath as well and tried to calm herself. Ben was right—she didn't want to fight with him, especially over her father. She felt a flash of irritation again. Even without being a part of her life, Jac Ludd was interfering in it! She couldn't understand why Ben was so obsessed with this, why it mattered so much to him. But she didn't want tension and hostility between them.

"I... I'll try. But I can't promise anything," she said. Then she gave him a tentative smile. "I just need to clear up a bit here, but when I'm finished— would you like to go and get a drink together?"

"Actually, I think I should join Craig and Dan— see if I can offer some moral support," said Ben. "But..." He hesitated and Natalie wondered what was bothering him. "Listen... Would you like to come over to my villa tonight?"

Natalie raised her eyebrows. "To your villa?"

Ben made an awkward gesture with his hand. "Yeah, it would be more private. We could order room service and have it out on the terrace. There's a great view overlooking the ocean."

"Sounds great," said Natalie. She smiled, thinking that she must have been wrong about him. Maybe he was just a bit tired. Or maybe she was just being overly sensitive and paranoid. His suggestion sounded wonderfully romantic. "What time shall I come?"

"How about eight?"

"I'll be there."

"Good. I'd better run and catch up with the other guys now. See you later." He hesitated again, then leaned forwards and gave her a swift, hard kiss. Then he was gone, covering the beach with great long strides as he hurried after Craig and Dan.

Natalie touched a finger to her lips. She turned

and caught Sara and Ellie staring, and blushed. But inside, she was secretly delighted at Ben's public display of affection for her. He couldn't have regretted the kiss, could he, if he was making it so clear to everyone now that he liked her?

"Milo! No! Bad dog!"

Natalie whirled to see the chocolate Lab cocking his leg against the side of the canopy.

"Hey! Milo!" She ran at him, flapping her hands. "Stop that!"

As Ellie grabbed the dog and pulled him away, Natalie wondered with a sinking heart what the ceremony was going to be like tomorrow with the unruly hound on the scene. Really, he shouldn't have been there. But she knew that Sara's offer to let Milo join in had meant the world to Will and no one had the heart to disappoint the little boy now. Well, hopefully it wouldn't be as bad as she thought... just as long as Milo didn't swallow the rings!

Natalie smoothed down the skirt of her dress as she stepped out of her car and locked the door behind her. She hoped she hadn't overdressed. She didn't want to look like she was trying too hard, although the truth was she had never tried so hard for a "date" before. She had spent ages with the curling tongs to get her hair into its current state of wavy splendour and taken more than usual care with her make-up, attempting to master the art of eyeliner for the first time in her life.

And—unable to find a suitably romantic outfit in her own wardrobe—she had finally succumbed to curiosity and looked through the small collection of her mother's clothes that her grandmother had saved. She had found this dress: a beautiful strappy number in deep wine red, with a slightly retro style—and it had fit her perfectly. In fact, when she had gone downstairs, her grandmother had gasped out loud and stared at her wordlessly for a moment. Rita hadn't said it, but Natalie knew that she was seeing Annabel again.

Natalie was surprised herself at how much her reflection in the mirror looked like the picture of her mother that Rita still kept by her bedside. But strangely enough, the resemblance didn't bother her like she thought it would. In fact, there was even a tiny flicker of pride in looking like such an attractive woman. Her mother had had a wild, fey beauty that had drawn many people to her. Natalie never thought she shared her mother's looks—but then, maybe she'd been trying too hard not to see it. Now, for the first time, she acknowledged that she was more her mother's daughter then she had previously admitted.

And perhaps that isn't such a terrible thing, she thought with a smile.

Slipping on a denim jacket, Natalie shouldered her handbag and walked slowly towards the main entrance. Then on an impulse, she turned and took a side route into the resort gardens which led around the main lobby building. The private luxury villas were all located at the back of the property and she could make her way there without going through the lobby and main areas of the resort. While it wasn't strictly forbidden for resort staff to have relationships with guests, there was no need to fuel gossip by having everyone see her heading to Ben's room dressed like this. She could just imagine Jean-Pierre waggling his eyebrows in satisfaction if the French chef saw her now!

The winding path led through the landscaped gardens—carefully cultivated to resemble the native Australian bush—past several private villas until, at last, it branched into two forks: the left leading down to the pool and the beach, and the right meandering farther into the undergrowth. Natalie took the right fork and walked slowly, enjoying the ambience. In the distance, she could hear the rush and murmur of the sea and she wondered how the canopy was holding up. Hopefully she had secured the drapes tightly enough against the sea breeze and wouldn't wake up to find the bamboo poles bare tomorrow morning.

She wondered how Craig and Sara were doing. She knew they were observing the tradition of not seeing each other the night before the wedding, but she did wonder if it might have been better to break the rule. They hadn't parted happily this morning after the rehearsal and she hoped that they had a chance to patch things up. So far as she was aware, the wedding was going ahead, but it would be a very uncomfortable atmosphere if they hadn't resolved their resentments by tomorrow when they would be walking down the aisle together.

Lighting at the resort had been kept chic and discreet. There were small beacon lamps carefully spaced out along the side of the pathway, nestled in the undergrowth so as to blend into the scenery. The little halos of light dotted along the ground gave the resort gardens a slightly magical feel. Natalie saw the row of lamps break ahead of her as a small side trail led off from the main path. The trail was marked with large stepping stones and led to one of the premium luxury villas. Built on a slight rise of land, it had a terrace which gave a sweeping view of the surrounding gardens and the beach beyond.

Natalie looked up and caught a glimpse of the raised terrace. There was a table with two chairs and a flickering candle throwing a soft, golden light on the gleaming wineglasses. It looked incredibly romantic and her heart thumped with excitement. Her mind jumped ahead to what the evening would bring. She remembered their passionate kiss at the cottage and wondered what would have happened if they had been here instead, alone, with no grandmother to chaperone them.

And what about tonight? What if Ben asked her to stay?

I'll stay. Natalie felt a shiver of anticipation pass through her. She had never been the kind of girl to jump into bed quickly with a guy; in fact, she was probably less experienced than a lot of girls her age. It might have been old-fashioned, but she had always felt that sex should mean *something*; that it should be an expression of love. She had never felt the urge to give herself completely to somebody... until now.

I'm in love with Ben, she realised suddenly. But instead of filling her with fear, as she had thought it would, she felt instead a sense of wonder, as if she'd stepped out into the light after too long in the dark. It was crazy and unbelievable and had happened in spite of all her resistance... but she couldn't fight it. She was in love with Ben Falco and tonight she was going to give herself to him.

CHAPTER TWENTY

Natalie walked up to the door of the villa, took a deep breath and knocked on the door. A moment later, it swung open to reveal Ben standing on the threshold. Natalie drew her breath in sharply. He was wearing a navy shirt with dark jeans, his open collar revealing a tantalising glimpse of tanned chest. He looked sexy and brooding and heart-stoppingly gorgeous.

"Hi..." She smiled shyly at him.

He smiled briefly. "Hi... Come in."

He moved aside to let her enter. Natalie stepped in and looked around in admiration. She had seen pictures of the luxury villas in the resort brochures, of course, but had never seen one in person. It was decorated in a rustic but contemporary style, with soft neutrals and warm timbers lending a cosiness to the spacious interior. There was a small foyer area, which led into the living room on one side and a hallway on the other. She could see floor-to-ceiling bifold windows along one wall of the living room, which opened onto the outside terrace. A glimpse of the beach showed through the foliage beyond the balcony: a pale blur of sand merging into the inky black sea. There was jazz music playing in the background and an open bottle of wine and two glasses on the living room table.

"Here, let me take that," said Ben, reaching out to draw her jacket gently off her shoulders.

Her pulse jumped crazily as he leaned close to her and his fingers brushed the bare skin at the nape of her neck. Goosebumps shivered over her skin. The air between them seemed to hum with desire.

"Thank you," Natalie murmured. She yearned to turn around and throw her arms around his neck; to ask him to kiss her again, the way he had done in the cottage. But she was too shy. In any case... she smiled to herself. They had the whole evening. No need to rush things.

"Have you been waiting long for me?" she said as she walked into the living room. "Sorry I'm a bit late. It took me much longer than I expected to get here—so much traffic on the freeway! Guess I'm not used to the roads coming in this direction at this time of the night. Usually I'm driving back to Summer Be—"

Natalie broke off as she realised that there was another person in the living room. He had been standing in the shadows of the far corner, which was why she hadn't seen him. But now he turned around and came forwards.

Her heart jumped into her throat as she recognised the craggy features of the older man moving towards her.

It was Jac Ludd.

The famous leonine mane was now streaked with grey and he was perhaps slightly shorter than he appeared when he was on stage, but there was no doubting that this was the notorious Jac Ludd, whose wild rocker lifestyle and stirring music had gripped the imagination of thousands of fans around the globe.

"Annabel...?" he said hoarsely, reaching out both hands to her.

Natalie jerked back.

"I'm sorry... you... you look so much like her." Ludd gave a slight shake of his head, as if to clear it. Then he spoke again: "Natalie?"

Natalie stared at him. She felt as if the room was spinning around her. Shock, horror, dismay, disbelief washed over her, combined with a deep sense of betrayal. She turned accusing eyes on Ben. He dropped his eyes, looking uncomfortable.

"Natalie..." Ludd came forwards again. "Sweetheart, this... this is a wonderful moment for me. You don't know how long I—"

"No..." Natalie staggered backwards, shaking her head. "*No!*"

"Please, I just want..." Ludd reached out and tried to catch her hand.

Natalie whirled and ran towards the front door.

"Natalie!"

She ignored the shouts behind her. Wrenching the door open, she ran out into the night, stumbling as she tripped over one of the stepping stones in her haste to reach the main path.

"Natalie!" A hand seized her arm and pulled her to a stop.

"Let me go!" panted Natalie, yanking her arm away from Ben.

"Natalie, please... Give him a chance," pleaded Ben. "Just give him five minutes,"

"How *could* you?" Natalie rounded on him, furious. "How could you have done this? Going behind my back and organising—"

"I didn't set this up on purpose! I got a message from Ludd when I came back to the resort yesterday morning, after I came back from your place. Your father had seen our picture in a magazine—the one the paparazzi got of us on the Woy Woy wharf. He recognised you and realised that you were with me. So he called me and told me how desperate he was to get in touch with you—"

"And you helped him."

Ben hesitated. "Well, yes. He had already decided to fly out to Summer Beach. All he asked for was the chance to see you, the chance to speak to you..."

"So you gave him that chance by tricking me into coming to your villa tonight," said Natalie bitterly.

"I wasn't tricking you! I really did want you to come—"

"How can I believe that? How can I believe anything you say to me now? How do I know it's not all part of some great ploy to soften me up?" Natalie demanded. "I suppose Ludd's promised to give you a great step up in your career if you acted as a go-between for him."

"What? My career has nothing to do with this!" Ben growled.

"Then why did you do it? Why should you care if I see Ludd or not?"

"Because he's your *father*!"

"I told you, I don't care! I'm not interested in anything he has to say—"

"That's because you don't know what it's *really* like *not* to have a father! You don't know what it's *really* like to have no parents—no family to belong to!" Ben was yelling now as well.

Natalie stared at him.

Ben took a deep breath and said, in a calmer voice, "You asked me the other day if my family lived near me in the States. The answer is no—because I don't *have* any family. I'm an orphan. I spent all my childhood moving from one foster home to another—and never feeling like I belonged."

He shook his head in despair. "You don't know how lucky you are to still have one parent there for you. I have never known my parents and I'm never going to have that chance now... while you throw your chance away so carelessly. I couldn't let that happen!"

"You could have asked me, instead of just going behind my back."

"I *did* try to ask you. I tried again and again to persuade you but you wouldn't listen."

"So you just decided for me, did you?" Natalie said angrily. "Well, I don't need you to sort out my life! In fact, I don't need you in my life at all!"

Yanking her arm out of his grasp, she turned and ran down the path, back towards the main resort buildings. After a while, she realised that there was no one coming after her and she slowed her steps. Hot angry tears started to her eyes, and she had to bite down hard on her bottom lip to stop them falling. She stumbled, wrapping her arms around herself and shivering in the cool night air. She had left her denim jacket at Ben's villa, but she wasn't going back for it. Thank goodness, at least she hadn't taken her handbag off—it was still slung over one shoulder and contained her car keys.

Natalie got back to the car and managed to slide in and slam the door before the tears overwhelmed her. She put her head down over the steering wheel as the sobs came, wracking her body. She didn't know what she was crying for—for the horror at

Ben's betrayal, for the loss of love, for the death of a dream... She remembered how excited and hopeful she had been when she had arrived at the resort, not even an hour ago. Her dress and hair and makeup seemed to make a mockery of her now. She grabbed some tissues from the glove compartment and scrubbed at her face viciously. Then she blew her nose, dried her eyes, and took a deep shuddering breath.

Gran mustn't know. She couldn't face the thought of going home now and dealing with her grandmother's questions and worried sympathy. No, she would have to drive around for a while, at least until it was late enough that her grandmother would hopefully be in bed and she could creep in unnoticed.

Natalie started the car and pulled out of the resort car park, heading for the freeway. She tried to push all thoughts of Ben out of her mind. *I've just got to get through the wedding tomorrow*, she thought. *Then he'll be going back to the States and I never have to see him again.*

And she tried to ignore the feeling of despair which filled her at the thought of never seeing Ben again.

CHAPTER TWENTY-ONE

Sara stared out the window of the luxury resort suite. Ellie had decided that it would be easiest to stay at the resort the night before the wedding, so that Sara could get ready on-site. So she had hired rooms for the whole wedding party, with the groom and other male members at the other end of the corridor, and this morning Mrs Monroe and Aunt Sophie had arrived early in Sara and Ellie's room to help the bride get ready.

Sara glanced over her shoulder. She could hear them chatting in the bedroom, where they were busy preparing the wedding gown and accessories. In a minute, the hair stylist and make-up artist would arrive to begin her transformation.

Sara turned back to look out of the window again. The sky was uncharacteristically grey this morning and it matched her mood. She couldn't believe that this was her wedding day, the culmination of weeks of dreaming and planning. She had thought that she would be nervous, happy, excited. Instead, she felt strangely flat. She knew it was because of the fight with Craig at the rehearsal yesterday. She hadn't seen him since then—they had spent the night apart as tradition dictated—and their last harsh words to each other had been eating away inside her.

I can't get married feeling like this, she thought wildly. *This is all wrong!* Suddenly, she realised that this day wasn't about the decorations or the cake or even how she looked in her dress. It was about her and Craig—and their feelings for each other. Without that, the rest was all meaningless. It didn't matter if the day wasn't perfect or if the media intruded a bit—all that mattered was that they were spending the day with each other, pledging a lifetime together.

Making a sudden decision, Sara turned and slipped out of the room. She hurried down the corridor in her bare feet until she reached the door of Craig's room. She knocked softly.

"Yes?" The door open and Dan looked out. His eyes widened as he saw Sara standing there in her towelling bathrobe.

"Can... can I see Craig for a moment?"

"Craig's actually just gone out."

"Where's he gone?" Sara stared at Dan in

surprise. "Shouldn't he be getting ready?"

"He said he needed some fresh air."

"Do you know which direction he went in?"

"Probably just around the corner, to the menagerie. He says Baz the emu always puts a smile on his face."

"Thanks." Sara turned away and hesitated for a split second, then turned and hurried to the lifts. She saw other guests staring at her, wide-eyed, obviously wondering what she was doing wandering around dressed only in a bathrobe, but she didn't care. She reached the ground floor and ran out quickly through a side door, taking the path that would lead her through the resort gardens to the enclosure which housed the small menagerie of rescued Australian wildlife. The pebbles on the path scraped her bare feet and the cold air seeped through her bathrobe, but Sara didn't slow her steps.

She rounded the corner and arrived at the enclosure—and saw Craig immediately. He was standing looking at the wallabies, his hand in his pockets, deep in thought.

"Craig?"

He spun around. "Sara! What are you doing here?" He came rapidly towards her.

"Looking for you." Sara shivered, pulling the edges of her bathrobe tighter around her.

"You're going to catch a cold, dressed like that," said Craig severely. "Temperature's dropped since yesterday. Do you want to be sick for the wedding?"

"*Is* there going to be a wedding?" Sara whispered.

Craig stiffened. "I was just wondering that myself." He paused, looking down, then said in a low voice, "Look, Sara... you can be honest with me. If you're having doubts or... if there's some... unfinished business, I'd understand. I don't want you to feel forced into this."

"No, no..." Sara shook her head vehemently. "Craig, I'm sorry... I don't know why I've let myself get so stressed over this wedding and the media and everything... I think I was losing sight of what was really important." She stepped closer to him. "I don't *care* about the stupid paparazzi or the TV show... and I certainly don't care about bloody Jeff Kingston!" She smiled hesitantly at him. "The only thing that really matters is us... and our life together."

Craig's face broke into a slow smile. He reached forwards and slid his hands around Sara's waist. "So I take it that you still want to marry me?"

Sara threw her arms around his neck. "Yes! Yes, I want to marry you, Craig—more than anything in the world!"

Craig laughed. Then he caught her mouth in a long, lingering kiss which left Sara breathless. At last, he broke the kiss and smiled at her.

"D'you know, I think that's the first time I've ever heard you say 'bloody'. You're sounding almost Aussie now, Miss Monroe."

"Well, since I'm about to become Mrs Murray, it's about time, don't you think?"

Craig threw his head back and laughed. "Too right." He caught hold of her hand and started back towards the main resort building. "So what are we waiting for? Let's go get married."

CHAPTER TWENTY-TWO

Natalie caught sight of her own reflection as she passed the mirrored walls in the resort lobby. Thank goodness she wasn't in the official wedding party, and no eyes would be on her during the ceremony. She looked awful. Her eyes were still puffy and red from last night's crying and her face was pinched and pale. Her grandmother had taken one look at her at breakfast that morning and demanded to know what had happened. It had taken all of Natalie's self-control not to break down in tears again. It was also the first time she hadn't confided in her grandmother. Things were still too raw at the moment. She couldn't face talking about Ben. She just wanted the whole thing to be over so she could crawl away and lick her wounds in private.

But today I've got a wedding to see to, she reminded herself. And Craig and Sara deserved to have the most wonderful day to remember. She felt an ache in her heart again as she remembered walking on the beach with Ben and telling him her dream of creating romantic, fairy-tale endings... Well, she might not have the fairy-tale ending for herself, but she was going to do a damned good job of giving it to others.

A few hours later, Natalie stood by the wedding canopy, making last minute checks. So far, everything had gone like clockwork. The guests had been arriving in a steady stream, chattering excitedly as they took their places on the wooden chairs laid out in a semi-circle on either side of the aisle. They exclaimed over the multi-coloured bamboo fans placed on each seat—delighted to find the wedding programme printed on the paper leaves—and admired the satin streamers tied to the backs of each chair, which fluttered gently in the breeze.

The TV crew and other paparazzi photographers had arrived early but Natalie was pleased to see that they were keeping a respectful distance, positioning themselves to the side of the chairs to get the best view of proceedings. She just hoped— for Sara's sake—that nothing which would be considered "good TV" would happen today!

She turned to look at the guests again and a delighted smile broke out on her face as she spied her grandmother and Graham, both looking uncharacteristically smart in their Sunday best. Natalie had been touched when Sara had called last night with an invitation for Rita and Graham to come to the wedding—as a small gesture of thanks for Natalie's hard work. Sara had even arranged for a limousine to pick them up from the cottage and it was evident from Rita's flushed, excited face that she had really enjoyed travelling in such style, and to be given the chance to attend such a glamorous event.

I must remember to thank Sara again afterwards—it was a really sweet thing for her to do, thought Natalie, turning to check the decorations on the canopy once again. It had been incredibly windy in the night and she had been anxious that she would wake up to find a rare gale had hit the coast and the carefully decorated canopy had been stripped naked... But after an ominous start this morning, the sky had lightened into a cerulean blue and the day had warmed up, almost rivalling yesterday's heat.

Now the sun was glowing low in the sky, turning the sea a deep shade of turquoise. The sheer white organza drapes on the wedding canopy looked beautiful against that vivid backdrop, billowing and flowing in the sea breeze. Fresh flowers had been added to the bamboo posts: clusters of frangipani and hibiscus in delicate pinks and snowy whites, touched by blush orange and soft lemon yellow and fringed with palm leaves. More frangipani had been scattered along the sandy aisle which was also lined on either side by starfish and seashells.

The whole scene looked like a magical beach fantasy and Natalie sighed with satisfaction as she surveyed her work. She could not imagine a more romantic setting to say "I do" than here, under that perfumed canopy, standing on the soft, white sand with the ocean in the background.

The tinkling ukulele notes from the intro of "Somewhere Over the Rainbow" drifted across the beach and a hush fell over the area. All the guests stood up and turned expectantly. Craig—looking very handsome in a cream linen suit, brocade silk vest, and bow tie—appeared by the side of the wedding canopy, accompanied by the best man. He took his position at the front of the aisle, his eyes riveted on the back of the beach where several figures were making their way down the path from the resort gardens.

First came Mrs Monroe, looking elegant in a chiffon tea dress, followed by the two bridesmaids, Pippa and Charlie, in their matching gowns of soft aqua silk. Then came Ellie, also in a silk aqua gown, beaming with as much pride as if it was her own wedding. Finally, as a reverent "Ahhhh..." went up from the audience, Sara appeared and walked slowly down the aisle on her father's arm.

She looked absolutely stunning—her honey blonde hair was caught up in a simple chignon at the base of her neck, with a few loose tendrils to frame her face. Clusters of delicate white and pink frangipani had been pinned into her hair behind her left ear, together with tiny starfish hair pins. A short veil, so thin it was almost gossamer, was affixed to the back of her chignon and trailed elegantly down her back. Her gown was in soft ivory, with a fitted bodice that moulded beautifully to the curves of her figure. The late afternoon sun caught the glitter of pearls and beading on the neckline and sleeves, and gleamed on the flowing folds of the silk skirt and train.

She walked in perfect time to the music and arrived at the front of the aisle just at the moment that Kamakawiwo'ole's soulful voice crooned the last words of the song. Her father handed her over to Craig and then everyone sat down as the couple took their place under the canopy.

"We are gathered here today in the presence of family, friends, and loved ones to witness and celebrate the joining of Craig and Sara in marriage..."

Natalie was surprised to feel a sudden lump in her throat as she watched the officiant say the familiar words. She swallowed hastily and blinked several times, turning slightly away from the wedding couple. Her gaze landed on Ben, standing on the other side of the canopy. Through a gap in the gently fluttering drapes, their eyes met and Natalie felt her heart give a painful jolt. She bit her lip and looked hastily away again, focusing on the TV crew instead who were carefully zooming in on the proceedings.

"...I, Sara Monroe, take you, Craig Murray, to be my husband, to have and to hold from this day forward, for better or for worse, for richer, for poorer, in sickness and in health, to love and to cherish; until death do us part..."

The couple were repeating their vows now, and then the officiant asked for the rings. Sara turned, smiling, towards the back of the beach. Will stood at the end of the aisle, looking very smart in a miniature tuxedo. Next to him stood a lady who was struggling to hold on to the two dogs. Coco whined, straining towards her owner, whilst Milo barked, bouncing up and down at the end of his leash.

"Coco... come!" Sara called.

The Beagle jumped forwards as she was released and trotted down the aisle. Everyone smiled and "*awwwed*" as they saw the little satin cushion tied to her collar with the two rings attached. The cameras turned and panned to follow the little dog.

Then there was a commotion at the back and the next moment, they heard Will yell:

"Milo!"

And the chocolate Labrador came barrelling

down the aisle after Coco. He caught up just as the Beagle reached the wedding couple under the canopy. Before anyone could stop him, he jumped on Coco and began to hump her head enthusiastically.

"Milo!" Ellie screamed in horror, rushing forwards to grab him.

"MILO! STOP THAT!" yelled Will, running down the aisle.

Flashbulbs went off as the paparazzi hurried to capture the moment and the TV crew ran in for a closer shot.

Oh hell.

Natalie looked at Sara in apprehension and saw Craig do the same. This was exactly the kind of wedding disaster and media nightmare that the bride had been dreading. Would she freak out again?

Then suddenly Sara began to laugh.

At first it was just a giggle, then harder and harder until she was clutching her sides, almost crying with laughter. Soon everybody was joining in, partly in relief and partly in sympathy. Even Natalie found herself chuckling. Okay, it was a pretty awful thing to happen in the middle of such a romantic ceremony and it did ruin her perfectly planned wedding, but then again… it was bloody funny! She didn't think she would ever forget the image of Milo—bounding down the aisle with his tongue hanging out and jumping onto Coco to the horrified screams of the audience—for the rest of her life.

At last, everyone calmed down and the dogs were safely leashed again, and the ceremony was able to continue. In a way, the mishap had lightened the mood and somehow brought people together. Young and old, Australian and American, everyone clapped and cheered as Craig and Sara finally turned around and walked back up the aisle as husband and wife.

CHAPTER TWENTY-THREE

Instead of going straight into the pavilion tent after the ceremony, Craig and Sara had decided at the last moment to have champagne and canapés served out on the beach first. This way, the guests could enjoy the beautiful sunset and have a chance to mingle more before sitting down for dinner.

The earlier music and the commotion with the dogs, not to mention all the TV crew and cameras, had attracted a lot of curious onlookers from among the resort's other guests. Although Natalie had cordoned off this section of the beach, it was not really "private" and any resort guest could walk down and join them. Most people, though, kept a respectful distance and only watched politely from afar, smiling and pointing at the "beautiful bride".

Natalie frowned as she suddenly noticed one

man drift closer than was really acceptable. In fact, as she watched in disbelief, he stepped over the cordon and marched up to the nearest waiter, helping himself to a flute of champagne. Her lips tightened in annoyance. This crossed the line from nosy onlooker to wedding gate-crasher!

Fuming, Natalie marched across the sand towards the man. He had turned, champagne in hand, and was now making a beeline for the wedding couple. He swayed slightly as he walked and Natalie realised with dismay—as she got closer and smelled the alcohol wafting from him—that he was already drunk.

"Excuse me, sir..." she called, reaching out to tap his shoulder.

"Gerroff me," he growled, pushing her away.

Natalie staggered back, only to find herself caught by strong masculine arms. She looked up. It was Ben.

"Are you okay?"

She nodded. She noticed that Ben still hadn't taken his hands away from her arms. "I think he's drunk," she said.

Ben frowned as he watched the gate-crasher. The man was almost at Craig and Sara now, and reached out to grab Sara's arm. She turned and colour drained from her face.

"Jeff?"

"Hey baby..."

"You've been drinking," said Sara in disgust.

"Hadda few onthaplane," Jeff slurred. "Gotta sherablate, right? Sherablate your wedding. Fine-ly manuj to catcha man, huh, baby? Guess he don't mindcha fat ass..."

Craig bristled and stepped forwards. "Watch your mouth, mate."

Jeff sneered. "Owat? Whatcha gonna do, ya kangaroo hick?" He gave an ugly laugh. "You musta lotta ugly beeches in Austraya if you're happy to take her—"

"You bloody bastard!" Craig said through clenched teeth and punched the American actor in the face. Screams rang out from the crowd.

Jeff Kingston reeled back, stumbled, then slumped onto the sand. More screams came and people surrounded him and the wedding couple. Ben rushed towards them, whilst Natalie turned urgently to the nearest waiter.

"Call security," she said tersely, before running to join the crowd.

Craig had his arm around a trembling Sara and was murmuring soothing words in her ear. He turned her away from the sight of her ex-boyfriend and started to lead her away.

Jeff Kingston picked himself up slowly and staggered to his feet. His face was a mask of fury. He raised his hand, which held the champagne glass, now cracked and broken.

"Aaarrrgghh!" he snarled, letting out a stream of swear words. He lunged towards Craig's back and raised his hand to stab with the broken champagne glass.

"LOOK OUT!" Ben jumped forwards and tackled the American actor, throwing him to the sand. The two of them rolled over and over, amidst more bellowing and cursing. More flashbulbs went off and the TV crew almost tripped over each other to get the best shot.

Natalie heard a scream and realised that it was herself. She watched in terror as Ben wrestled with the drunk man: he was completely unarmed and he had nothing to defend himself with as he dodged the jagged edges of the broken glass. A gasp went up from the crowd as Jeff slashed viciously and Ben jerked back with a grunt of pain. A bright red stain appeared on his arm. Jeff gave a jeering laugh and lunged again.

A sudden volley of barking came out of nowhere and then a dark shape burst out of the crowd. It was Milo. The Labrador bounded up to the two men, barking excitedly. Natalie didn't know if he was playing or attacking, but the big dog jumped on Jeff, knocking him flat on his back.

"Ruff! Ruff! Ruff! Ruff!" barked Milo, mauling Jeff enthusiastically.

"Aarrrgghh! Unn…uuggh!" Jeff struggled to push the dog off his chest.

"He's going to cut Milo!" screamed Will, running forwards.

"Will!" Ellie grabbed the boy and pulled him

back.

Then suddenly two beefy men in uniforms were there. They grabbed Jeff Kingston and hauled him to his feet, removing the broken glass from his hand. Milo barked even more excitedly and bounced in a circle around them. Natalie ran across to Ben, who was getting slowly to his feet. Her heart lurched as she saw that he was holding his right arm with his left hand, grimacing with pain.

"Ben! You're hurt!" She grabbed his right arm and pushed back the sleeve to see the slash on his forearm. Blood was oozing from the wound.

Sara hurried over. "Oh my God, Ben..." She stared, round-eyed, her hand over her mouth.

"It's all right—it's not deep," Ben reassured Sara. He gave a wry smile. "Honestly, I make my living with my hands—my career would be dead if I couldn't play a guitar—so if I thought this was serious, I'd be rushing myself to the nearest hospital."

Sara shook her head. "Still—"

"I've got a first aid box in there," said Natalie, gesturing to the pavilion. "Come on, we need to clean it and stop the bleeding..."

"Sir..." One of the uniformed men approached Ben. "When you're done, would you answer a few questions for us? The authorities will need to know the details in order to arrest—"

"It's okay. I'm not going to press charges," said Ben.

"Are you sure, sir?" The security guard raised his eyebrows. He nodded at the wound on Ben's arm. "Kingston is certainly guilty of assault and there are multiple witnesses."

Ben glanced at the TV and paparazzi cameras all trained on him, then he looked at Jeff Kingston, his clothes dishevelled, his face bruised and his nose broken, being supported by the other security guard.

"Yes, I'm sure. Just get him out of here," he said.

Sara gave him a grateful smile.

Ben turned to her and Craig. "Go on... don't worry about me. You've got a bunch of guests here and everybody is shaken up. Go sort it out. Don't let that jerk ruin your wedding."

Craig gave his shoulder a squeeze. "Cheers, mate."

"And give that dog a pat from me," added Ben with a smile, nodding at Milo, who was now back by Will's side. The Labrador was sitting with his tongue hanging out, looking extremely pleased with himself as people hovered around him and made a fuss of him. "I think he saved the day."

Natalie led Ben to the pavilion, trying to ignore the photographers who followed them, snapping pictures along the way. At least the paparazzi had the decency to stop following when she ushered Ben into the pavilion tent and dropped the flap. She closed her eyes for a second, letting out a breath of relief at the peace and quiet around them.

"This is turning out to be some wedding, huh?"

She opened her eyes to see Ben giving her an ironic smile. Hysterical laughter suddenly bubbled to her lips.

"Sorry," she gasped, trying to hold it in. "I know I shouldn't laugh—"

"Better laugh than cry," said Ben, grinning. "And when you look at it, it's pretty damned funny in a way."

"Oh my God, the paps are going to have a field day! And the TV crew! They must be stoked. They couldn't have done better if it had all been scripted. This is like ratings gold."

"I actually think Milo is going to get his own TV show after this," said Ben, chuckling.

Natalie led him over to the first aid box, which was by the stage, and Ben sat down on the edge of the stage whilst she crouched next to him. Carefully, she cleaned the wound and bandaged it, noting with relief that the bleeding had stopped already. When she finished, she didn't take her hands away immediately, letting her fingers linger instead on his arm.

In the distance, they could hear the faint sounds of conversation and laughter coming from the wedding party and the even fainter sounds of waves crashing onto the beach... but here in the dimly lit pavilion, she was suddenly aware of how alone they were. She flashed back to the first time they had met and how she had also crouched down next to him to tend to an injury.

As if reading her mind, Ben said softly, "Funny how you always seem to be rescuing me."

Slowly, Natalie raised her eyes to meet his. Her heart began pounding in her chest as she saw the expression in his eyes.

"Natalie..."

His hand covered hers, his fingers strong and warm as they laced with hers. He pulled her gently towards him and she found that she couldn't resist. Everything that had happened the night before, all the things that had been said, faded away now. Nothing mattered but this moment in time. Ben leaned forwards... closer... closer... and touched his lips to hers. Natalie trembled as he kissed her with heart-breaking tenderness. Then he lifted his head and looked at her.

"Natalie..." he said urgently. "I'm sorry about last night. I never meant to hurt you. I thought I was doing the right thing... but I was wrong. I should have tried to put myself in your place and tried to understand how you feel about your father. It was wrong of me to interfere and I—"

"Shh..." Natalie pressed a finger to his lips, shaking her head.

He stopped, bewildered. "I'm trying to explain..."

"I don't want you to explain."

He stiffened.

Natalie smiled. "I want you to kiss me again."

Ben stared at her for a moment, then he pulled her roughly into his arms and his mouth came down on hers. Tentatively at first, then harder and bolder; he kissed her with a hunger that set her heart racing. She found her own arms sliding around his neck as she kissed him back with all the pent up emotion she had been carrying inside. Hot and urgent, they kissed and clung as if they were never going to let each other go.

At last, they broke apart and leaned back slightly, each breathing fast. Ben reached out and tenderly brushed a tendril of hair back from her forehead. He started to say something, then they heard a voice from outside announcing that it was time for the guests to head in to dinner, followed by the sound of people moving towards the pavilion.

"Maybe we can continue this conversation later..." Ben said regretfully.

Natalie squeezed his hand. Then she got up and hurriedly began packing up the first aid box. "Yeah, I'd better go and check on the cake. We don't need any more dramas!" she laughed.

CHAPTER TWENTY-FOUR

Natalie needn't have worried. The dinner and speeches went without a hitch and when the cake was finally brought out, everyone gasped and *oohed* and *aahed* in admiration. Jean-Pierre had outdone himself. The wedding cake was a breath-taking creation decorated with rich buttercream and marzipan shells and seahorses. He had cleverly blended whole Tim Tam biscuits into the design and also created alternating layers in a mix of different flavours: vanilla, chocolate fudge, and caramel. At the top, in pride of place, was a Tim Tam tower in the shape of a heart.

Milo raised his nose eagerly as the cake was rolled past the table where he was sitting with Will. He eyed it greedily, pulling on his leash.

"Watch that dog!" someone called out and

everyone laughed.

Craig escorted Sara up to the cake and the guests clapped and cheered as they cut it together.

Then Sara turned around and said, with a twinkle in her eyes, "I think I know who deserves the first piece."

She cut a huge wedge from the vanilla layer, placed it on a plate and took it over Milo. The Labrador could barely contain himself, his tail wagging furiously, as she put the plate down on the floor in front of him. He hesitated, looking at her as if unable to believe his good fortune, then at a word from Will, he jumped forwards and gobbled up the cake.

Everyone laughed again and more cake was passed around and coffee and tea served. The lights were dimmed as Ben stood up and went to the stage, where a band was waiting for him. Craig and Sara walked smiling onto the middle of the dance floor and, as the music started, slowly began to dance. Everyone stopped and watched them. They were so beautiful to watch, their eyes on each other, their bodies moving in perfect unison as they circled the dance floor. Sara's gown swirled in rich folds around them and the pearls and beads in her hair gleamed in the lamplight.

Natalie sighed with happiness as she stood to one side, watching them. *This* was the fairy-tale ending she had always dreamt of... and it was wonderful to feel that she had had a hand in making it come true.

Then Ben began to sing and Natalie felt her breath catch in her throat. His voice was deep, slightly rough, and incredibly sexy. She couldn't take her eyes off him. When she finally tore her gaze away to look at the crowd, she saw that everyone else seemed mesmerised by him too. There was that quality in Ben's voice—a raw, emotional edge—that made you feel as if he was singing only to *you*.

The first dance ended and Ben started a new song—this time with a thumping bass beat that got everyone's toes tapping. People sprang up and joined Craig and Sara on the dance floor.

"He's awesome, isn't he?" Ellie said to Natalie as she skipped past, dragging Dan with her. "I love this song! It's from his latest album!"

Ben sang song after song—hits from his own albums as well as popular favourites—and people bobbed and shimmied and swayed and jived in time to the music. Natalie was caught up in the festivities as well, as Craig grabbed her hand and twirled her into a dance. Then Dan grabbed her, then Matt, one of the other vets from the Summer Beach Animal Hospital, and even young Will took a turn. She was swung around the dance floor until she was dizzy and breathless. Yet all the time she was dancing, she was aware of Ben's eyes following her as he crooned into the microphone.

At last there was a lull in the songs and Natalie thought that perhaps Ben might take a break. He'd definitely earned it. She wondered if he might come down and join her—maybe they could have a dance together at last whilst the band played an instrumental number. But to her surprise, he stepped up to the microphone again, this time holding a guitar.

Her mother's guitar.

"I'd like to sing this for someone special here tonight."

An expectant silence fell over the room.

Ben began softly plucking the guitar and a soulful Latin-style tune with a sensual tempo filled the air. Natalie recognised the song. It was "Could I Have This Kiss Forever". She stood in the middle of the dance floor, staring at him, her heart thumping in her chest. The lyrics from the song washed over her as Ben sang of looking in her eyes and how she had captured him, of wishing that the night would never end. She felt as if everyone had receded and it was just the two of them in the pavilion. Ben never took his eyes off her as he sang, his velvet, throaty voice bringing goosebumps to her skin.

Natalie didn't know when she had moved, but suddenly she found herself by the side of the stage. As Ben began the second verse, she climbed up and walked over to stand beside him. One of the band members held out a microphone and Natalie hesitated for a second, then her fingers closed around the stem and she raised it to her mouth. She met Ben's eyes and began to sing.

Everyone in the pavilion watched, mesmerised, as the two of them sang of holding each other close for a lifetime, of sharing a kiss forever, their voices rising and melding in perfect harmony. When the final notes of the song died away, there was a hushed silence for a moment, then the whole room erupted with cheers and applause.

Natalie flushed with exhilaration as she faced the crowd. She caught a glimpse of her grandmother in the far corner, dabbing her eyes and beaming. It would be the first time Gran had heard her sing in years, she realised. And she also realised suddenly that she felt as if a huge weight had lifted off her shoulders. She felt as if she had been released from some terrible burden, awakened from a heavy daze. She glanced sideways at Ben and the guitar he held in his hands. Her mother's guitar.

And she thought of the man who had flown halfway across the world to see her. Of the pain in his eyes when she had flinched from him and screamed at him and ran away.

She leaned towards Ben and said in his ear, "Where's Jac Lu—where's my father?"

He looked at her in surprise. "He's gone back to the States. I saw him off this morning. I insisted that he go immediately—I didn't want him to upset you again."

"Oh."

Natalie felt something strange stir in her chest, something that felt almost like... regret. She shook off the feeling and smiled at Ben. "I haven't had a dance with you yet."

"Then I'd better do something about it," Ben said with a wink.

He held his palm out and she put her hand in his, then he led her off the stage and onto the dance floor. People smiled and called out to her as she passed.

"Natalie! That was incredible!"

"I didn't know you could sing like that!"

"Wow, Natalie—that's some voice you've got there."

Natalie paused as she came suddenly face to face with her grandmother.

"Gran..."

Rita Walker beamed and held out her arms. Natalie stepped into them and hugged her grandmother close.

"Thank you," her grandmother whispered. "You've given Annabel back to me tonight."

Natalie felt a lump come to her throat and she squeezed her grandmother tighter for a second, then stepped back. Ben tugged her hand gently and pulled her into his arms on the dance floor.

The rest of the room faded away again as they twirled slowly together. Ben held her close, one hand possessively against the small of her back, the other clasping her hand against his heart. She could feel it beating fast in his chest. He lowered his head slightly, so that his lips brushed her forehead and she felt a shiver of pleasure at the caress.

"Natalie..."

"Yes?"

"My flight leaves tomorrow."

Natalie felt her stomach drop. Her hands clenched tighter around his. "So soon?"

"I have to get back to start working on the next album."

"Yes, of course..." She tried a bright smile. "But, as the cliché goes, we've still got tonight."

"Is that all we have?" He looked down at her, his eyes intent. "Is that all you want? Because I want more—much more. As the song said, I want this night to go on forever."

Natalie stared up at him, her heart pounding. What was he saying?

Ben laughed softly. "I know this sounds crazy... we've barely known each other for a week, but... sometimes the way these things happen *is* crazy. All I know is... I'm in love with you, Natalie Walker."

Natalie felt as if her heart was going to burst out of her chest. "I'm in love with you too, Ben Falco," she whispered. "I think I fell in love with you the day you washed up on the beach covered in jellyfish tentacles."

Ben laughed out loud, and Natalie joined in. He spun her wildly around, until Natalie was squealing, then he pulled her close and kissed her hard. Whoops and cheers went up from the crowd around them. Natalie broke the kiss and looked around, blushing.

"I think we're stealing the attention away from Craig and Sara," she said.

"Well, then let's do it properly," said Ben with a wicked gleam in his eye. He stopped dancing and dropped to one knee, catching both of her hands in his. "Natalie, I've been wanting to ask you this for a while. Will you..."

Natalie drew a sharp breath in. *Surely he wasn't going to...?*

"... come back to America with me?"

A slow smile spread over her face. "Yes, I will. Yes!"

CHAPTER EPILOGUE

(Two weeks later)

Horns blared, brakes squealed, and everywhere was the sound of people talking, talking, talking, the clamour of a huge metropolitan city. Natalie stared wide-eyed around her as she followed Ben down Park Avenue. They slowed as they arrived at the front entrance of an imposing brownstone. The uniformed doorman smiled at them as he held open the door and they stepped into the elegant foyer, lit by a small chandelier.

Ben walked up to the bank of elevators and pressed the call button. A minute later they stepped into the luxurious elevator car. As they ascended to the soft hum of machinery, Natalie nervously checked her reflection in the wall mirrors.

"Do you think I look okay?"

Ben smiled at her. "You look beautiful."

The elevator arrived with a ping and the brass doors slid open. Ben began to step out, but Natalie clutched his arm.

"Wait!"

He looked at her in surprise.

"What if... what if he doesn't like me?" Natalie asked.

Ben leaned close to her and whispered, "He loves you already." Then he pressed a tender kiss to her temple and held out his hand. "Ready?"

Natalie took a deep breath, then smiled. "Ready."

She slipped her hand into his and, together, they stepped out of the elevator. They turned down the hallway and walked towards the door of the apartment where an old man was waiting to finally meet the daughter he loved.

THE END

Don't Forget to Check Out The Other Books in this Series:

Summer Beach Vets: Playing for Love (Book 1)
Summer Beach Vets: Playing to Win (Book 2)
Summer Beach Vets: Playing by Heart (Book 3)
Summer Beach Vets: Playing the Fool (Book 4)
Summer Beach Bride: Seaside Duet (Book 5)

To be notified about new releases, as well as special deals, and other book news, join the mailing list here:
http://www.hyhanna.com/newsletter

AUSTRALIAN SLANG GLOSSARY

Arvo - afternoon

Aussie – a person from Australia (pronounced "Ozzie") or an adjective for something that is Australian (e.g. "Aussie animals")

Barbie - barbecue

Beauty – great, fantastic, showing excited approval (often used in the phrases "You little beauty!" or "That's beaut!")

Bloke – man (equivalent to "guy")

Bloody – known as "the Great Australian Adjective", not regarded as profane or swearing, it is used as an intensifier for both positive and negative qualities (e.g. "bloody awful" and "bloody wonderful")

Bloody Nora – exclamation of surprise and horror, similar to bloody hell, often used by women

Bluey – depending on context, can refer to: 1) a redhead 2) a bluebottle jellyfish 3) a Blue Heeler cattle dog 4) a traffic ticket 5) a type of blanket taken into the Outback

Brekkie - breakfast

Bugger – not considered an insult or derogatory term; the meaning depends on context: often used as a term of endearment ("you old bugger") or sympathy ("poor bugger") – although sometimes used to describe someone or something that is annoying ("he can be a little bugger") or to express derision ("what a rotten bugger"). The word by itself is also frequently used as an exclamation to express surprise, frustration, exasperation or disappointment: "Oh bugger!"

Chinwag – a chat, a conversation

Cozzie – swimsuit (short for swimming costume)

Crikey – an exclamation of surprise or bewilderment

Don't get your knickers in a twist – don't get worked up and upset about something

Drongo – an idiot

Flaming Galah – an idiot, a fool OR a loud, rudely-behaved person (after the bird called the "galah", a native Australian cockatoo that's very noisy)

G'day – the ubiquitous Australian greeting
Loo – toilet

Maccas - MacDonald's

Maggoty – angry, bad-tempered

Mate – friend, sometimes equivalent to "buddy"

Medico – a medical professional, usually a doctor

Me – sometimes used instead of "my" (e.g. "I've lost me socks")

No worries – no problems, don't worry about it, that's all right

No biggie – no big deal

Op – operation OR opportunity (depending on the context)

Oz – Australia

Paps – paparazzi

Poncey - pretentious

Postie – postman

Rapt – very happy

Ratbag – a troublemaker

Ripper – fantastic, very good

Roo - kangaroo

Sook – a soft, wimpy person; easily upset

Spunky / Spunk – an attractive person of either sex

Stinger – jellyfish

Stoked – very happy & excited about something

Strine – Australian slang, based on the way Australians pronounce "Australian" = "Aus-strine"

Sunnies – sunglasses

Take a squizz – take a look

"Tall poppy" – highly successful people who rise above the rest and may develop an overblown ego. They are often seen as needing to be "cut down" in Australia, where the culture favours the "underdog"

Thongs – flip-flops

Too right – vehement agreement with something

Tucker - food

Uni – university

The following Australian words are not "slang" but the meanings may be unfamiliar in American usage:

Car park – parking lot

Chips – fries (deep fried potato sticks)

Crisps – chips (thinly sliced potato snacks in packets)

Takeaway – takeout

C.V. – curriculum vitae (usually referred to as a resumé in the U.S.)

Vegemite – a dark brown food paste (usually used on bread) made from brewers' yeast extract with various vegetable and spice additives. An iconic Australian food—people either love it or hate it!

OTHER BOOKS BY THE SAME AUTHOR:

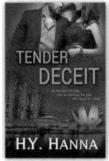 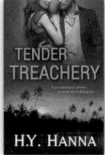 

 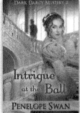  

Please visit the author's website to see her other books:

www.hyhanna.com

ABOUT THE AUTHOR

H.Y. Hanna is an award-winning author who writes mysteries, sweet romances and romantic suspense, as well as children's fiction. After graduating from Oxford University, she tried her hand at a variety of jobs before returning to her first love: writing. She has won awards for her novels, poetry, short stories and journalism.

After graduating from Oxford University, Hsin-Yi tried her hand at a variety of jobs, including advertising, marketing and ESL teaching, before returning to her first love: writing. She worked as a freelance journalist for several years, with articles and short stories published in the UK, Australia and NZ, and she has won awards for her novels, poetry, short stories and journalism.

A globe-trotter all her life, Hsin-Yi has lived in a variety of cultures, from Dubai to Auckland, London to New Jersey, but is now happily settled in Perth, Western Australia, with her husband and a rescue kitty.. You can learn more about her and contact her at: www.hyhanna.com.

ACKNOWLEDGMENTS

As always, I am so grateful for the support and encouragement from my amazing husband—who not only does everything he can to give me more time to write, but also patiently endures endless discussions on plot conflicts, the colour of the hero's eyes, and is even reading romantic novels for the first time in his life!

Printed in Great Britain
by Amazon